a FORTUNATE BLIZZARD

L.C. CHASE

RIPTIDE
PUBLISHING

Riptide Publishing
PO Box 6652
Hillsborough, NJ 08844
www.riptidepublishing.com

A Fortunate Blizzard
Copyright © 2015 by L.C. Chase

Cover art: L.C. Chase, lcchase.com/design.htm
Cover Photo: Jenn LeBlanc/Novel Expression
Editor: Danielle Poiesz
Layout: L.C. Chase, lcchase.com/design.htm

ISBN: 978-1-62649-340-7

First edition
November, 2015

Also available in ebook:
ISBN: 978-1-62649-339-1

A FORTUNATE BLIZZARD

L.C. CHASE

RIPTIDE PUBLISHING

There are few things in life as transcendent as that one perfectly random connection with another human being that has the power to change the course of one's life.

CONTENTS

CHAPTER ONE

"*I* know this is hard, Trevor," Dr. Wheyvan said. She gave him a tight smile, then turned to rummage through a cabinet drawer behind her desk.

Trevor took a deep breath and stared up at the human anatomy poster on the wall. How many times had he sat right here, studying that poster while waiting for Dr. Wheyvan to come into her office? Every time hoping she had good news for him. Every time leaving with an increased sense of time running out as the fringes of his optimism grew a little darker.

"We can't give up hope yet," she said, spinning back in her chair, a sad smile on her lined face. She held out a pamphlet. "But the reality is such that you should be prepared."

He took it from her and sighed. Gold letters on a blue background read, *Deciding to Stop Dialysis. What You Can Expect.* His throat tightened and the letters began to blur. He inhaled the stale, sterile air that seemed universal to doctors' offices and held his breath, fighting back tears that no longer had the right to run down his cheeks.

It was always going to come to this, wasn't it? He'd already used more than his fair share of life's allotted good luck.

Seven years he'd been on dialysis waiting for a kidney transplant. Seven years he'd been trying to keep hope alive and shiny. Seven years he'd been fighting something he could only slow down.

He nodded. "You told me from the beginning that it would be a long shot because of my blood type."

"A long shot is still a shot," she said.

But long shots were finite, and ready or not, he could feel his coming to an end.

"If I decide to go off dialysis . . ." He swallowed with difficulty. "How much time am I looking at?"

"It depends on several factors—age, lifestyle, ESRD complications that arise, et cetera. You've always taken very good care of yourself, so you may have more time than others." She studied him for a second, and he knew he wasn't going to like what she was about to say. "Generally anywhere from four days to, at most, two weeks."

Four to fourteen days? His throat closed, vision narrowing in on the pamphlet in his hand, yet he couldn't see it.

He didn't look up. "And if I stay on it?"

"If a transplant doesn't come through in the next six months . . . Maybe a year."

The gut punch stole his breath, and a cold chill spread over his skin. If Dr. Wheyvan was still speaking, he couldn't hear it over the ticktock of mortality's stopwatch, booming like thunder in his ears.

"Trevor . . ." Her warm, comforting hand on his shoulder drew him back from the edge of panic. He forced himself to look up, focus on the compassionate eyes that told him he wasn't alone.

Dr. Wheyvan had been with him since day one. Through all the tests, all the treatments, all the hopes and letdowns of desperately trying to find a match that would save his life. She'd be with him at the end, too.

"Nothing needs to be decided now," she said, her voice soothing. "You're still so young, and you're as healthy as you can be, and medicine keeps advancing."

"Thirty-nine is not that young. That's pretty much midlife."

"Since when are you a glass-half-empty kind of man?" Her smile didn't reach her eyes, but he appreciated the gesture. Even so, he could only shake his head in response.

Dr. Wheyvan frowned. "You've got time, Trevor."

"Not much," he said, the words tight and threatening to choke him.

Her smile faded, and her eyes began to shine. He looked away. If she started crying, there was no way he'd be able to hold back his tears. This wasn't new or unexpected, only a reality he'd been hoping would go away if he ignored it long enough. That if he prayed hard enough, his match in shining armor would appear, save his life, and he'd live happily ever after.

He snorted. Everyone else was out looking for his or her prince, and here he was searching for the prince's kidney. "None of us know how much time we have left—a week, a year, ten years. All we can do is make the most of what we've got right now," she said quietly. "And right now, I want you to go home and enjoy the holidays with your family and friends."

With a nod, Trevor stood and pulled her into a brief hug. "Merry Christmas," he choked out, and then spun on his heel, exiting her office without looking back.

Five minutes later, he stood outside the doctor's office, zipped up his jacket, and turned his face to the pale-gray Boulder skies. Light snowflakes brushed over his exposed skin like feathers, falling in a lazy dance until they came to rest, quiet and gentle, at his feet. Would this be his last winter? His last Christmas?

This wasn't how it was supposed to go. He wasn't supposed to be thinking about "putting his affairs in order" before he reached forty. He should be sharing his life with a handsome, charming man and thinking about settling down now that marriage equality had finally become the law of the land, not contemplating how he wanted to die.

A familiar chime drew his thoughts from the mental wishing well, and he pulled his cell phone from his pocket. Closing his eyes, he took a second to gather himself before swiping his thumb over the screen to accept the call.

"Hey, Mom," he said, grateful he'd managed a cheerful tone. Shoving his free hand in his pocket, he turned and began walking to the parking lot, puffy clouds formed by his breath leading the way.

"*Mi cariño.* How did things go with your doctor today?" The subtle lift of hope in her voice poked at his heart. She'd stopped asking if they'd found a donor a couple of years before, but she couldn't completely tamp down her unwavering hope. He'd lost track of how many times they'd held each other while she'd cried, helpless and angry that she couldn't save her son from this. But very few people could, and of those, even fewer were willing.

"Good," he said, hoping to blame the tightness in his voice on the cold air pricking at his skin and freezing his eyelashes. "Nothing new. Nothing that can't wait to tell you in person."

Nothing he wanted to voice over the phone right now—or *could* voice. The news was banging around inside his head in such a chaotic fashion that he couldn't even begin to articulate it.

Her brief pause told him she was fighting the urge to demand he tell her right now. She usually pressed when she knew he—or anyone in his family, really—was holding something back, but she also knew when to let things go.

"I saw on the news that there's a blizzard warning there," she said instead, and he sent a silent thank-you to the universe. "They've already started canceling some flights into Denver. I want you to catch an earlier flight before they shut the airport down."

"Okay, but I need to get to my treatment right now. I'll call and check right after." Reaching his car, he pulled the keys from his pocket, unlocked the door, and climbed inside, immediately turning over the engine and cranking the heat. "But you know we're built for snow here. It'll be fine."

She huffed. "Nothing is built to withstand Mother Nature in a snit. Call me when you have your new arrival time, and we'll see you at the airport."

Trevor had to smile. His mom refused to take no for answer, no matter who or what dared to stand in her way. "I will."

"Do it now, right after you hang up."

"Yes, Mom."

She laughed, and he surprised himself by joining in, halfhearted as it felt to him. But as long as she didn't pick up on it, he could get through the rest of the long day ahead. He was going to have to talk to her and the rest of his family about what options he had, limited as they were, but that conversation could wait until after the holidays. Maybe if he put it off long enough, it would just go away. He could stick his head in the sand and pretend he was perfectly healthy, pretend his kidneys were miraculously getting better rather than worse. That he had years and years ahead of him, that he'd see his nieces and nephews grow up, that he'd find his soul mate . . . that he wasn't facing the decision of dying comfortably on his own terms now, having lived a good life, or dying later, after his body deteriorated to the point that he simply existed in painful misery until his inevitable end.

"I love you, *mijo*," his mom cut in to his thoughts, as if knowing he'd slipped down the path to Maudlinville.

"All we have is today," she'd told him time and again. *"Live it."*

He still had now, he reminded himself. Tomorrow he could think about how many "nows" were left.

"I love you, too. See you tonight."

He put his phone away, grabbed his snow scraper, and got back out to clear off the windshield. Only then did he notice how much snow had accumulated during the hour of his appointment. Quarter-sized flakes were falling at a steady pace, the sky a solid off-white slate, and a good four inches of fresh powder already covered the roof of his car. If it kept up, he might not make it to the airport at all, let alone have to worry about canceled flights. Luckily, he'd already packed, so he wouldn't have to run back home up the mountain after his treatment. At least there was one good thing about this day.

"Come on, Prince Charming," he said aloud, his breath bursting into the air on tiny white clouds. "All I need is one of your kidneys. Just one."

CHAPTER TWO

"*M*arcus Roberts!"

Startled, the affidavit he'd been reading fell from his hands. He looked up to see Kate Bellamy standing in his office doorway with a scowl on her face. Her usually pulled-back dark hair now hung loose and long around her shoulders.

"Third time's a charm," she said, sauntering in to stand in front of his desk, hands on her hips. Her narrow gaze focused on the files scattered about his desk.

He frowned, retrieving the paper he'd dropped. "What do you mean?"

"I had to call your name three times to get your attention." She plucked the page from his hand and began gathering up the loose papers on his desk, placing them unerringly into their respective files. With barely a glance, she seemed to know which went in which folder. A prime example of the many things that made her one of the best paralegals at Rawlings, Frank, and Earnhart, Colorado's most prestigious law firm.

"Oh, sorry." He reached for a file folder, and she batted his hand away. "What are you doing?"

"*You—*" she pointed at him with a piece of paper "—are going home."

He leaned back in his chair, watching as she neatly stacked the folders. Kate had always made a point of telling him he was the last person in the office when she left for the day, a subtle hint that he should leave as well, to which he'd crack a joke and she'd walk away shaking her head, even as she laughed. But she'd never outright told him to leave before. He didn't know whether to be annoyed at the order or touched by her concern.

"I've got hours yet until my car turns into a pumpkin," he said with a smile.

She shot him a leveling stare and then motioned to the bank of windows behind him. "Look outside and tell me what you see."

With a sigh, he obliged. Kate had joined the firm a little over three years ago, and he'd quickly come to rely on her expertise and knack for doing the impossible. He'd had a pretty solid track record with the firm over the ten years previous, but it had been flawless since she'd come on board. Which meant he wasn't going to piss her off and essentially lose his right arm.

Outside, the short daylight hours of winter had given way to slate-gray darkness as white flakes drifted steadily down. "It's snowing. Surprise, surprise."

"Smart-ass," she said, a note of laughter in her voice. "Look again."

This time he looked beyond the snow to the city below. His office was on the seventh floor, facing west. Usually he could see the Front Range stretching north to south beyond the city, but now he could barely make out buildings he knew were only blocks away. Snow had already begun falling as he'd driven into work that morning—it was winter after all—but he'd had his head down all day, so focused on a new case he'd picked up from another attorney that he hadn't realized how much had accumulated.

"That's a lot of snow," he said, turning to face her.

She raised an eyebrow. "That's practically Snowmageddon, and they've issued a blizzard warning. Most everyone has left for the holidays already, and you need to get home before you get snowed in."

He shrugged and offered a playful smile. "If I do, I can hit the gym downstairs, and then have dinner at the diner."

"If they're even still open. And then what? Sleep on your office floor?" She shook her head and leaned down to retrieve his briefcase from beside the desk.

"Why not? It'll save me the commuting time, and I can get more work done." With the new case added to his already heavy workload, he wasn't kidding about using the time to make some headway. It wasn't like there was anyone waiting for him at home anyway.

Kate set his briefcase on the desk and began stuffing his files into it. "You do realize tomorrow is Christmas Eve, don't you?"

"Of course!" Actually, he hadn't, but there was no way he'd admit that to her. That the holidays were upon him had danced around the edges of his consciousness, but he'd ignored it. The same way he had for close to twenty years now. All Christmas did was serve to remind him he hadn't been a good enough son in his mother's eyes. That he wasn't the star academic or athlete that his brothers had been was the least of it—his mother finding out he was gay, too? He'd become a living ghost in his own home from that point on. So yes, he deliberately pushed the festive season from his mind as best he could, buckled down, and focused on work until the holidays passed and life got back to business as usual.

Judging by the concerned look Kate gave him now, she didn't believe him. She dropped the last folder into the briefcase and snapped it shut with a bit more force than necessary.

She let out a breath, as if collecting herself before speaking, her voice soft when she said, "Please tell me you're not spending the holidays alone, Marc."

"I'm not spending the holidays alone." Another lie. He smiled, hoping it didn't appear as fake as it felt.

"I know we don't talk much about our personal lives, and I really don't mean to overstep here, but . . ." She sat down in a chair in front of his desk. "I worry about you."

His eyebrows shot up. Whatever he'd been expecting, it wasn't that. He was a grown man, perfectly capable of taking care of himself. Had been ever since his eighteenth birthday when his mother unceremoniously shoved him out the door and into the great big world all by himself. Longer than that even. She'd wiped her hands of him for good that day, but he'd already ceased to exist in her eyes years before.

"Why on earth would you worry about me?" A terrible thought entered his mind, and a chill slithered into his chest. "Did the partners say something?"

"No! No. Nothing like that." She raised a hand in a placating gesture. "It's just . . . This workaholic thing you do isn't healthy."

"I'm not a workaholic." He frowned, even as relief that the partners weren't displeased with his work flowed through him. Was he a workaholic? He was working hard toward a goal, to proving himself, sure, but that was called being focused and disciplined.

"Marc," she said, her tone stern, "you're the first one in the office and the last one out, every single day. You don't take breaks, you work through lunch, and you're always taking on extra cases. In all the years I've worked with you, not once have you taken a sick day or a vacation day. You never join me and the guys after work for drinks or dinner . . . You don't even stop for watercooler chat."

True, but he had good reasons to limit his socializing. "I'm on track to make partner by spring, which means putting in a ton of hours. You know what it takes. I don't have the time for anything else right now." Not only was he on a fast track, but he was going to be the youngest partner in firm history, and he wasn't going to do anything to jeopardize that.

"There's more to life than making partner."

"Not for me," he blurted. He quickly looked away. He hadn't meant to say that aloud and hoped she didn't press for him to explain.

"Being so driven is admirable, don't get me wrong," she said, and he gave silent thanks she let his comment go. "But not at the cost of everything else in your life."

"It hasn't cost me anything."

"Really? What happened to Tony?"

Marc sighed and rubbed a hand over the back of his neck. She knew damn well what had happened to Tony. He'd come into the office to see Marc, but Marc had been on a call with a client. Instead of waiting until his call ended so they could talk, Tony had given Kate a message to deliver. Their five-month relationship was over because he was tired of Marc's work always coming first. Granted, Marc did work a lot and had canceled more than a few of their dates because things had come up or run longer than planned. It wasn't always going to be that way, but that didn't matter to Tony. *Don't call* had been his final words to Marc, scribbled on a pink "While you were out" message pad.

"Things will change after I make partner," he said quietly, but deep down he knew that wasn't true, either. As partner, he'd only have to work harder. He couldn't blame Tony for leaving.

"Will they?"

"Okay! Okay!" He laughed, raising his hands in surrender. "I give. I promise to get a life."

"Good to hear." Seemingly pleased she'd gotten through to him, she stood and walked over to a coatrack behind his office door.

"After I make partner," he added.

Kate groaned, rolled her eyes, and shook her head. "Go home. Take your suit off and put on some real clothes. Tell me you own a pair of jeans."

"I own more than one pair," he teased.

"Shock of all shocks! Now go." She handed him his jacket and briefcase, and gave him a gentle shove toward the door. "Be festive, have merriment, and build a snowman."

He couldn't help but laugh. Him, build a snowman? That was never going to happen.

"C'mon," he said after he pulled on his jacket. "I'll walk you out. Can't have you missing Christmas because you got held up trying to get my sorry ass out of here."

.

CHAPTER THREE

"*I* should have stayed at the office," Marc grumbled, his voice echoing inside the empty car.

It'd been three hours since Kate had shoved him out of the office, and the only thing that had moved on the Boulder Turnpike was his gas needle, inching its way toward empty. He sighed and dug his cell phone out of the center console. No missed calls or texts. No one who would worry or check up on him, stranded out in the worst blizzard to hit the Rocky Mountain Front Range and eastern Colorado in over a decade.

He hadn't worried when the snow had started falling earlier that morning. Denver knew how to deal with snow, and it never slowed anyone down for long. But this was close to two feet in twice as many hours, with snowdrifts as high as eight feet. According to the radio, CDOT closed the highway between Boulder and Golden because the drifts were nearly twice that. The road crews just couldn't keep up.

If Kate hadn't checked in on him, he'd still be at work—stuck there and having dinner from the vending machine. Now here he was, gridlocked on the turnpike somewhere between Denver and Boulder, with hundreds of similarly stranded, disgruntled commuters. Soon his car would run out of gas and he'd be forced to tough out a night in the freezing cold.

His stomach grumbled, and he added "starving" to his growing "Joys of Being Stranded in a Blizzard" list. Attempting to distract himself from his body's plea for sustenance, he scrolled through his phone contacts. There was Kate's number, and several numbers for each of the senior partners from the firm. Not that he'd ever called them for any reason beyond work. He also had the numbers for three of his favorite restaurants—since he never had the time nor the inclination to cook meals for one—the number to the gym where he worked out religiously every morning, and . . . his mother's number. He stared at it blankly, his thumb hovering over the Call button. How many times had he wanted to press it, to try opening that long-closed connection, only to shove the phone back in his pocket? Hadn't she made it clear enough all those years ago that she was done with him, that he didn't measure up to her standards?

Swiping his address book closed, yet again, he dropped the phone back into the console and stared out the window. The thick, rhythmic sway of falling snow was hypnotizing. As unimpressed as he was at being trapped on the turnpike, he had to admit the snow was beautiful to watch—peaceful in its silence, tranquil in its insistence that the world stop and take a breath, release its grief, cleanse its soul, and start anew.

Kate was right. His quest for partner, on making something of himself and becoming someone his mother could be proud of, had cost him. Friends, relationships, and most of all, his true dreams, had fallen by the wayside of his single-minded drive for professional success. But he was almost there. Just a little longer and then he'd have the time to get serious about finding someone to share his life with.

Yeah, you keep telling yourself that, Roberts.

A shiver charged up his spine, scattering his thoughts.

"Damn snow," he muttered, because blaming his sour mood on the weather was easier than looking any deeper for the real source.

He turned his attention to the line of vehicles ahead in hopes of seeing any kind of sign that traffic would start moving again soon. It looked like something out of a postapocalyptic movie. *"Snowmageddon,"* Kate had said. Just a long line of frozen vehicles for as far as the limited visibility would let him see, which wasn't farther than a few hundred feet. A silent and still world, all its inhabitants long gone except for him. A strange sense of loneliness crept into the back of his mind, and he quickly shoved it away.

A knock on his window startled him, heart pounding against his ribs from the jolt. A state trooper stood outside, so bundled up Marc wasn't sure if it was a man or woman. He rolled the window down, just enough to speak through, while his pulse settled back down. Cold air charged inside the car, slamming against his face and pulling a shiver from him.

"Turnpike's shut down in both directions." A man's voice, muffled by the scarf covering his mouth and nose. A gossamer puff of steam from his breath obscured the rest of his face with a ghostly effect.

"No hope of getting out of here tonight, then?" Marc asked, wishing again he'd ignored Kate and stayed at the office.

"Where's home?"

"Boulder."

The trooper shook his head. "Afraid not." He pointed across the turnpike. "We're not far from Superior, though, and there's a hotel just off the turnpike there."

Marc followed the line of the man's gloved finger to see a dim yellow halo of lights in the distance. People were heading in that direction—hunched, dark blotches moving slowly against an otherwise solid blanket of dancing white.

Damn it. Barely ten miles from home but it may as well have been a thousand.

"Doesn't look too far," Marc said. And he did have a change of clothes and toiletries in his gym bag in the trunk. He could spend the night in comfort and warmth instead of freezing his ass off in the car for who knew how long.

"Maybe a half-hour trek in these conditions." The trooper may have shrugged his shoulders, but he was so bundled up that Marc couldn't be sure. "I'd encourage heading over there for the night, if you're able. It'll be safer and warmer until the blizzard passes and we can get traffic dug out."

Marc's office attire wasn't all that conducive to trudging through a couple feet of snow, but at least he could bury himself in his work when he got to the hotel.

He glanced at the dashboard. The gas needle slipped down to an eighth of a tank, making the decision for him. He'd need enough fuel to get off the highway when the road crews were finally able to clear the way. Whenever that would be.

Marc nodded. "I think I will do that, thanks."

"Good call." The trooper rapped on the roof of Marc's car a couple of times. "Wait for me to check in with the vehicle ahead of you. I'm trying to send people in groups for safety."

"Will do," Marc said and rolled up the window. He grabbed his winter jacket, scarf, and gloves from the backseat, and pulled them on before opening the door. Cold air dug into his skin like a million razor-sharp fingernails. In the seconds it took to walk to the back of the SUV, open the hatch, and grab his duffel bag and his briefcase, his eyelashes and the fine hairs in his nostrils had already frozen. Sitting down in the driver's seat again, car door still open, he swapped his slick-soled dress shoes for running shoes, slung his things over his shoulder, and then joined his assigned companions for the trek across the frozen tundra.

A little over an hour later, after securing one of the last rooms at the hotel and a much-needed, very long, and very hot shower to thaw his frozen body, Marc sat in the crowded hotel lounge for a late dinner. His table was at the back, but tinted glass walls let him watch as more disgruntled, snow-covered people stumbled into the hotel looking for warmth and shelter for the night. The soles of wet shoes squeaked on the polished marble floor as people crossed the lobby to the reservations desk, and white flakes drifted from heavy jackets and knit hats, leaving small puddles in their wakes. The place was a mess.

Marc reached for his hot brandy, but paused with the glass halfway to his lips when a tall man crossing the lobby caught his attention. He didn't look much different from the rest of the popsicle people at first glance, but something about the way he stood, the set of his broad shoulders, and those thick muscular legs wrapped in worn denim made Marc sit up a little straighter. The loneliness he'd been feeling earlier perked up too.

"If there is a god . . ." His whispered prayer trailed off when the man glanced toward the lounge and bright-blue eyes skimmed past him.

The man stepped up to the desk and reach into his pocket. His mouth lifted into a smile Marc wished he could see straight on instead of in profile. The man's hand stalled, shoulders dropped infinitesimally, and his stance shifted from one of confidence to one of defeat. If Marc were in the courtroom, that change in an opponent's body language would have been his cue to go in for the kill and win the case. But right now, it told Marc what he already knew. *No rooms left at the inn, son.*

CHAPTER FOUR

*T*revor's shoulders slumped when the young clerk told him they were booked solid. "This day just keeps getting better."

"I'm so sorry, sir." The clerk's dark eyes shone with genuine sincerity. "People have been coming in all evening, and with the airport closed now too, we filled up fast. You're more than welcome to spend the night in our lobby or lounge. We're gathering as many extra rollaways, blankets, and pillows as we can find, and the kitchen won't be closing tonight."

He forced a smile. "I guess that will have to do, then." Not that he had any choice in the matter anyway. Not when the airport shuttle he'd finally caught had pulled into the hotel parking lot, and the driver announced they wouldn't be going any farther. "Thank you."

Trevor walked back into the main lobby area and pulled his cell phone from his pocket. His mom was going to kill him for not taking her warning about the snow seriously.

"*Cariño.* Did you catch an earlier flight? Please tell me you caught an earlier flight and you've just landed." The words were rushed, her accent coming through stronger than usual, and his heart ached at the tentative hope in her voice. He would be spending Christmas alone for the first time in his life.

"No, I didn't. I'm sorry, Mom." Trevor sighed and sat on the arm of a vacant chair. "The airport is completely shut down. Traffic is gridlocked from the snow, and people are stranded everywhere."

"Oh, *mijo.* Where are you now?"

"The shuttle dumped us at a hotel off the turnpike, but it's fully booked." A cold gust of air swept over him as the doors opened to let more stranded people inside.

"You can't get back home?"

"Nope. No one's going anywhere, so I'm stuck here for the night, at least. I was on the phone with the airlines for a while, and it looks like there's no chance I'll make it home for Christmas. I'll be lucky if they manage to book me on another flight the day after."

His mom was silent for a moment before she quietly said, "It won't be the same without you, *cariño*."

"I know." He ran a hand through his hair, pushing the bangs out of his eyes. God, he was getting tired. He hadn't felt too bad after his treatment, but the day was quickly catching up with him—and it looked like it was going to be a long one. If only there were still rooms and he could lie down for a while and recharge.

"Well"—her voice was stronger now, an edge of determination to it—"we'll wait until you get here."

"No! You can't do that to the kids and everyone else. Especially Isaac. He'd have a fit." His mom let out a short bark of laughter, but she couldn't argue that point. Isaac was the same age as Trevor was, but when it came to everything Christmas, his brother acted more like three than thirty-nine. Trevor loved that infectious effervescence, though, and would never dream of dampening it. Not if he could help it. "Have Christmas. We'll just have to celebrate extra big on New Year's."

A soft sniff echoed down the line, causing his eyes to sting and throat to tighten.

"Mom, it will be okay," he said, fighting to keep the emotion from his voice. If he didn't, then the two of them would both break down and his dad would have to step in.

"But what are you going to do? I feel horrible thinking of you all alone out there. Without your family. It's not right."

"Your little boy is not so little anymore," he quipped, hoping to inject a little levity into the situation. "I think I'll be okay."

She huffed. "You'll always be my baby boy, even when you're an old married man."

"Yeah." Trevor squeezed his eyes shut and sank down into the seat of the chair. He was never going to be old or married, as much as he'd love to be both. But he wasn't about to burst his mom's bubble of hope right now. "And you'll be the most gorgeous mother of the groom the world has ever seen."

"Have you met my future son-in-law yet?"

"No, Mom. Not yet." And he wasn't going to, either. How could he start any kind of future with someone when he didn't have one of his own?

"Well, you'd better hurry up before your mama is too old to look sexy in her high heels while she walks you down the aisle."

"If he's out there," he mumbled.

"Of course he is!" Her adamant tone triggered an unexpected sense of loss for something he was now more certain than ever he'd never have.

Silence settled on the line between them, and over the din of the busy hotel lobby, Trevor heard laughter in the background. A rush of homesickness hit him hard. Should he move back home for his last days? As much as he wouldn't want to put that on his family, after all they'd given and done for him, he knew his mother would kill him for even letting the thought that they'd think him a burden wander through his mind.

"Okay." He gave himself a shake, hoping to dispel the creeping fatigue. "I'm going to go get some hot food and find a chair for the night. I'll give you a call when I get my flights rebooked. Give everyone a hug for me."

"I will. I love you." Her voice caught on a hiccup. "We'll miss you."

"I'll miss you, and love you, too. Talk to you soon."

Trevor ended the call, dropping the hand holding it to his knee and bringing his chin to his chest. He would be okay, he knew that, but the prospect of spending the holidays by himself cast a dark pall over his mind. All his friends had either left town already or had their own families in the area. Even if the blizzard let up in time, he didn't want to intrude on anyone else's holidays. Missing his own family, coupled with the reality of his future, such as it was, deepened the emptiness that was trying to consume him. The last thing he wanted was for his mood to bring down anyone else.

A heavy sigh pushed past his lips as he shoved the phone back in his pocket, grabbed his bag, and made his way into the lounge.

The place was quickly approaching standing room only, and Trevor had to shoulder his way up to the bar, where he ordered a tea with lemon—because the Irish coffee he really wanted wasn't worth the damage it would do to his kidneys—and a plain buffalo burger with a small side salad. The bartender slid a steaming cup in his direction and the first sip made Trevor's eyes water, sending a rush of heat cascading outward from his stomach. He closed his eyes, and he might have moaned but couldn't be sure over the chatter of voices surrounding him.

"Perfection," he said under his breath.

The barkeep smiled and shook his head. "Be 'bout fifteen minutes for your burger."

"Thanks."

Trevor dug a pill pack out of his bag, popped the two binders he was to take before every meal, and then turned his sleep-weary eyes on the lounge at large, scanning for an empty table. Through the crowd, he caught sight of a vacant seat at a table in the far corner. He leaned to the side for a better look and froze when his gaze locked with one of the most attractive men he'd seen in a long time. He had classic good looks: strong jawline, dark hair trimmed neatly, eyes that somehow seem brighter than they should in such dim lighting, no matter their color.

The back of Trevor's neck and his face began to heat as the man held his stare. Whether it was from the tea or the intensity of those eyes boring into him, he couldn't say. And he couldn't look away. The handsome stranger managed to hold him captive without word or touch. That kind of instant attraction was rare for him, and of course it had to happen *now*, when he had nothing left to give anyone.

Though . . . a little temporary comfort was still allowed, wasn't it?

Someone moving through the packed lounge jostled Trevor, spilling his drink and breaking his heated connection with the man across the room. He turned away, skin sizzling from head to toe and hand burning from the hot tea.

"Order's up, buddy." The bartender slid Trevor's dinner across the bar top.

Trevor jerked his head up. "Already?"

The barkeep just did that smiling and shaking his head thing again as he grabbed a towel and wrapped it around a handful of ice cubes. He set the faux ice pack beside the burger.

Trevor had to shake his head, too—mentally anyway. Had he and Mr. Handsome really been locked in a staring contest for fifteen minutes?

"Thank you."

The barkeep nodded and went back to mixing drinks. Trevor rubbed the soothing ice pack over his burned skin until the sting eased, and then turned around, his gaze instantly reconnecting with Mr. Handsome across the room.

Without breaking eye contact, Handsome reached over and angled the empty chair away from the table in silent invitation.

You'd be a fool to ignore that, Trev.

He shouldered his bag, picked up his plate and what was left of his tea, and made his way across the lounge. "Mind if I join you?"

A sensual smile stretched Mr. Handsome's lips, his forest-green eyes sparkling. "Please."

His deep voice sent a shiver of excitement up Trevor's spine, and he cleared his throat. "Thank you." He tucked his bag under the table and pulled up the chair. "This is a lot more comfortable than trying to eat at the bar."

"More elbow room," the man said. He motioned toward Trevor's bag. "Were you heading for the airport?"

Trevor nodded and reached for his drink to wash down the bite of food he'd just swallowed. "I was on my way to Connecticut to spend the holidays with family."

"I can't believe they actually shut down the airport." The man paused to take a sip of his drink. "When was the last time that happened?"

Trevor's gaze lowered to the mouth of the sexy stranger sitting across from him, following the way his full lips curved over the rim of the glass, the way his Adam's apple bobbed as he swallowed. A sudden image of those lips around something else rose in his mind, sucking, swallowing, and . . .

Shit, get a grip.

Trevor shifted in his seat and dropped his focus to stare pointedly at his food. "I'm not sure it ever has," he said, a rough edge to his voice. "Bad timing too, with the holidays and all."

"Will you be able to get another flight?" the man asked, seemingly unaware of Trevor's quick trip to a mental porn set.

He shook his head. "Looks like now I get to spend it alone in Nederland."

"I'm sorry to hear that." There was something in the man's voice that made Trevor think he could relate. Then dark eyebrows rose and a flirty smile, intentional or not, sent a little thrill dancing in the back of Trevor's mind. Damn, but this man was attractive.

"You live in Ned?" Mr. Handsome's tone was playful. "You'll be lucky to get back up there before March."

Trevor laughed. Yes, living at eighty-two hundred feet did have its drawbacks, but he couldn't imagine living anywhere else. There was an intangible energy in the mountains that soothed his soul and fed his creative muse. He hadn't achieved critical success as an artist until he'd moved here, even though his mom always said he was so talented he'd have reached that level anyway, regardless of geography. Nederland wasn't all that out there in the boonies, either—just a thirty-minute drive down into Boulder . . . when the roads weren't covered in snow. Chances were high the canyon road would end up closed from the blizzard too, if it hadn't been already.

"It suits me." Trevor shrugged. "How about you?"

"I was on my way home from work in Denver. Got stuck on the turnpike. Home is Boulder."

"Wow. We're practically neighbors." Trevor took a bite of his burger, and his tablemate's gaze focused on his mouth, staring long enough for heat to infuse Trevor's cheeks before he lifted his eyes to meet Trevor's. The air between them simmered and buzzed over the surface of his skin.

Damn. And he'd thought he was getting tired? Suddenly he was feeling fresh as a new day.

He put his burger down and struggled to swallow. Jeez, when was the last time he'd been so enticed by someone he'd just met? And when was the last time his body had shown even a spark of interest since he'd been diagnosed? Sure, he'd experienced instant attraction before, but he could count on one hand the number of times his breath had caught and his heart had stuttered. Which would be exactly one time. Now.

He reached out across the table. "Trevor."

The hand that engulfed his was warm, smooth, and confident. "Marc."

They shook twice, but Marc held on to Trevor's hand instead of letting go right away—or maybe it was the other way around. Regardless, he didn't care. The feel of Marc's skin against his pinged every nerve ending with teasing jolts of pleasure, nudging at desires long ignored, and he fought the urge to lick his lips.

"Pleasure to meet you, Marc," he said, his voice husky from the low hum of arousal coursing through his veins.

"Pleasure's all mine." Marc's green eyes gleamed, and a hint of a grin tipped up the corners of his mouth.

A long beat or two later, Marc released Trevor's hand slowly enough for his fingertips to slide along Trevor's palm. Imagined on his part or forward on Marc's, the effect was the same. Trevor's previously dormant libido was waking up, and right then and there, he wanted Marc.

CHAPTER FIVE

"Can I get you two another drink?" A frazzled-looking waitress interrupted their heated stare. Trevor leaned back, not having realized that he'd bent forward in the first place, pulled into Marc's intense eyes by some unseen force.

"Not for me, thank you," he said.

"I'll have another hot brandy, please," Marc ordered. With a nod of her head, the woman turned on her heel, and then they were alone again. Well, as alone as they could be in a packed lounge.

Marc shifted in his seat. "So what do you do, Trevor?"

"I'm an artist. And you?"

"Lawyer."

"Oh no!" Trevor exaggerated a wince, and Marc laughed. "There has to be a joke somewhere about that. An artist and a lawyer walk into a bar . . ."

Marc chuckled. "With the number of 'walk into a bar' jokes out there, I wouldn't be surprised if there is one."

"I'm going to have to google that now," Trevor teased.

Charged silence settled between them for a long moment, and their eyes locked again. Trevor knew he wasn't imagining it, seeing his own desire reflected back at him in captivating shades of green. He had zero intention of starting anything with anyone, but there was no denying the way this man was tripping all his wires. They were two grown men stranded in a blizzard, though. What could it hurt to enjoy each other's company for one night? Assuming Marc had been able to get a room, of course.

"So . . ." Marc began. He looked down at his drink briefly, as though he were carefully choosing his words or about to admit some deep, dark secret. Trevor caught the slight dip of Marc's mouth as he pursed his lips, making a dimple in his cheek peek out. Uncertainty flickered in those eyes like a passing shadow, and gave Trevor the impression there was a story behind Marc's outward confidence. A story he suddenly found himself wanting to hear. Or better yet, paint.

"Tell me what life as an artist is like." Marc absently slid a long, manicured index finger around the rim of his glass.

Trevor followed the movement, hypnotized. A flush spread over his skin, seeped beneath the surface, and hopped a ride on the fast-moving current of blood in his veins to pool in his groin like an oasis at the bottom of a waterfall. Christ, all he could think about was getting Marc alone.

He cleared his throat and lifted his eyes. A faint grin tipped one side of Marc's mouth, and Trevor fought the urge to lean across the table and capture those lips with his. Marc lifted an eyebrow, expectant. He was waiting for . . .?

Oh right, an answer. And the question was . . . not what he'd expected. He really had thought he was going to hear some sort of confession, and now the simple question about his work threw him off.

Floundering, he cleared his throat and blurted, "I paint."

Marc's grin stretched into a full-on smile and transformed him from merely attractive to heart-stoppingly gorgeous. "I've heard a lot of artists do that." He winked.

Trevor laughed, a self-conscious weak-sounding thing, and ran a hand through his hair, tongue-tied. When did that ever happen?

"Well, no two days are quite the same, which suits me fine." Aside from his dialysis treatments, which were as regular as clockwork. "I spend a lot of time observing the world around me, drawing and painting how I see it, how it makes me feel, what I hope my interpretation gives to others. Nothing makes me happier than being able to create something that moves or inspires someone in a positive way."

"That sounds like a beautiful life," Marc said, a wistful note in his voice.

Almost. He knew he had a lot to be grateful for, knew he was fortunate to be able to make a living doing what he loved most in the world. There was just that little ticking clock that dulled everything around the edges.

Trevor shrugged. "I can't complain." He smiled and received a matching one from Marc. The slow spread of it, the softness and promise in it wrapped around Trevor like a security blanket.

Amid the hustle and bustle of the bar, an easy stillness settled between them. Voices, laughter, and music teased Trevor's hearing, and people dancing and making the most of their snowbound evening blurred in his peripheral vision. A bubble seemed to have formed around the small table in the back corner where they sat, protecting them from the world mere feet beyond them.

"How about you, Mr. Lawyer?" The low, husky tone didn't surprise him, unintentional as it was, but the fire that flared in Marc's eyes in response had Trevor sitting up a little taller. "Are you some high-powered shark defending criminals like the ones I see on TV?"

"God, no." Marc shook his head. "I like to think I'm one of the good guys. I'm a civil rights attorney."

Trevor raised his eyebrows, his thoughts immediately turning to a sexy Matthew McConaughey, who once played a lawyer defending a black man in the deep South. But now his mind's movie reel replaced Matthew with Marc. "Tell me more."

"It's not nearly as exciting as it looks on TV." Marc grinned, and his eyes sparkled. "Mostly it's just a lot of paperwork and research, preparing arguments and such."

"What about in the courtroom?"

Marc shrugged. "There can be some drama, but the high-profile cases don't really come around all that often."

"So what kind of cases do you handle, then?" Trevor leaned forward, drawn in by Marc's soothing, seductive voice. Didn't seem to matter what he was saying as long as he was simply speaking.

"Let's say, for instance—" Marc paused, and Trevor got the feeling it was cut for effect "—that you're gay."

The effect worked, and Trevor grinned. "Go on."

Marc tipped his head slightly and complied. "The state of Colorado has laws in place that protect employees in the private sector, as well as at state- and local-government levels, from discrimination based on sexual orientation, and gender identity and expression. Let's say again, that a video of your boyfriend proposing to you . . ."

Trevor's smile stretched wider, and he shook his head. Twice. Slowly. "Single."

Marc nodded, the light in his eyes brighter. "The video goes viral, your boss sees it, and after fifteen years of being a model employee, fires you for no reason other than that you're gay. I'm the guy you want at your back to settle those situations."

"I'll have to remember that," Trevor said, deliberately dropping his voice an octave. "And . . . I think I would like having you at my back."

The man was flirting, and the images that rushed into Marc's mind of him at Trevor's back had him acutely aware of his cock shifting in his pants. A strong naked back, Trevor moaning and writhing in his arms as he plunged deep . . .

He might actually have to thank Kate for kicking him out of the office.

Marc certainly wasn't looking for any kind of relationship, but enjoying another's company for one night wouldn't interfere with his climb to partner. And if he was reading Trevor right—and he was certain he was—maybe they could make the most of being snowed in. Trevor hadn't been able to get a room, after all . . . and Marc had one ready and waiting.

For now though, sitting here talking with Trevor was like being on vacation, as though he had nowhere to go and nothing to do but simply sit and enjoy the day and the company. He liked the way Trevor's long-fingered, graceful hands moved as he talked, the way his smile shone through his eyes, and Marc found he wanted to know more about him.

"Tell me about your art," he nudged. "What is your favorite medium and style? What inspires you?"

Trevor chuckled, his sky-colored eyes ablaze, as though the sun shone in their depths. "Are you sure you really want to get me going?"

"I am." *Because in another life I'd never have become a lawyer.* "I've always admired artists."

"So . . . you have a thing for us creative types?" Trevor teased.

A pink blush colored his cheekbones, but he didn't shy away from Marc's gaze.

"Something like that." Marc smiled. He couldn't deny he was feeling something for this particular one right now, but he was interested for more reasons than that. Interacting with people like Trevor gave him a chance to brush against something he'd given up years ago—to live vicariously, if only for a moment. "Was art something you always knew you wanted to do?"

"I've been drawing and painting for as long as I can remember," Trevor said, the focus of his eyes going distant as though reliving a fond memory. "My parents encouraged me to explore and develop my interests and talents. One of my earliest memories is of my mom coloring with me."

A pang of envy and loss struck Marc with surprising force. Hadn't that been what he'd wanted once upon a time? How different would his life have been if . . . *No.* He mentally shook those thoughts from his mind. He wouldn't be the highly successful lawyer he was today if the course of his life had been any different.

"You're lucky to have had that kind of support," Marc said, fighting to keep his voice casual.

Trevor nodded, lifting a hand briefly, his finger pointing—or more like flicking—in Marc's general direction. "Believe me, I know how much I lucked out when my parents chose me."

The comment struck Marc a little odd—maybe he was adopted?—but he didn't press. He sipped his brandy and let Trevor's voice drift over him.

Their conversation moved seamlessly from topic to topic, though time seemed to stand still. Which made the yawn that threatened to crack Marc's jaw a shock. Caught off guard as he was, he couldn't cover it fast enough.

But Trevor didn't seem offended, going by the amused glint in his eyes and his playful smile. "I agree. It's been a long day."

"Indeed." Marc glanced at his watch, surprised to see they'd been sitting there for the better part of three hours sharing their life stories. He hadn't noticed the crowd had thinned out, either. It was still busy, but no longer standing room only. Those who hadn't found rooms were either pulling all-nighters or curling up in corners with extra hotel blankets and pillows. "Well, I suppose we should call it a night, then."

Trevor's face seemed to fall ever so slightly. His lips parted as if to speak, but the follow-through never came.

"Did you manage to get a room for the night? I think they filled up pretty fast." Marc already knew the answer, but he asked anyway. Didn't want Trevor to know he'd been watching him ever since he stepped through the front doors.

Trevor shook his head. "I'll be roughing it somewhere in the lobby tonight." The faint inflection on that last word very nearly made Trevor's comment a question, and a wave of hope crossed his features, splashed over the table, and began to fill up Marc.

Marc held Trevor's gaze. "I have a room."

A glass clinked and someone laughed boisterously, but the cacophony was muted, just low enough to register but not loud enough to actually decipher. All Marc could focus on was the hunger—and not of the empty-stomach variety—radiating from the man across from him. Marc was certain if he looked close enough he would see tiny bursts of blue-white energy snapping and exploding between them.

"It has a king-sized bed. You're welcome to share it with me. Uh . . . the room, I mean. I'm pretty sure it has a rollaway." Where the hell had those nerves come from? *Jesus.*

Marc resisted the urge to tug at his tie, only then remembering he'd taken it off earlier after he'd checked in. They'd been sparring innuendo all night, so he was sure Trevor knew where this was leading, but still, he didn't want to be presumptuous. He pulled at his watch strap. "At the very least you can get a hot shower and a proper night's sleep."

"I—" Uncertainty crossed Trevor's features, and he looked away for a second.

Maybe he'd been reading Trevor all wrong.

But then the sides of Trevor's mouth tipped upward and his eyes darkened when they once again met Marc's. "I'd like that. Very much."

His voice, deep and husky, had Marc's desire beelining straight to his groin. "Thank you."

Marc nodded, then cleared his suddenly dry throat and downed the last of his drink. "Shall we, then?"

Trevor's smile widened, and the air crackling between them grew louder. "Lead on."

Marc stood and shoved his hands into his pockets to stop them from trembling. It wasn't like he'd never had a hookup before, but this felt . . . different somehow. Why, he couldn't say. Maybe it was because the few hookups he'd experienced had involved a nightclub, liberal amounts of alcohol, and minimal conversation before coming to a mutually beneficial release. This time he'd spent hours getting to know Trevor, and he'd enjoyed every second of it. Enjoyed it so much that, shockingly, if Trevor really did just want to sleep on the rollaway, he'd still be happy to have Trevor's company for the night. Well, mostly.

Trevor gathered his bag and jacket and stood facing Marc, waiting for him to show the way. Again, that invisible current snapped between them, pulling at Marc and burrowing a little deeper under his skin, sinking into his bones. Trevor moved aside and placed a hand on the small of Marc's back, guiding him forward. That tiny, gentle touch stole his breath and awakened his senses even more.

Hyperaware of Trevor behind him, the nearness, the heat of him, Marc caught the leg of a chair with his foot and stumbled. A firm grip on his biceps kept him from tipping past his center of gravity. *Jesus, Roberts. Pay attention!*

He shot a quick glance over his shoulder, hoping Trevor wouldn't notice how red his face must be. This was *not* like him. He didn't get flustered over men, he wasn't klutzy, but for whatever reason, here he was, fumbling around like a high schooler on a first date.

This is not *a date*, he reminded himself quickly. *This is a hookup. Period, full stop.*

"Thanks," he said.

Trevor nodded, an amused grin on his face, but he didn't drop his hand from Marc's arm until they stepped out into the lobby. The release was slow, like a caress, and a tingle lingered in its wake.

They walked side by side in silence, shoulders brushing, anticipation and excitement sparking in the atmosphere surrounding them. They paused at the elevator doors, and Marc took a deep breath. This time he knew where his nerves came from: he hated elevators.

Steeling himself, he reached out and pressed the Up button with a slow, shaky finger.

"I take it you're not a fan of the vertical lift?" Trevor asked, pointing to Marc's unsteady hand.

He shook his head. "I never take elevators."

"Ever?" Trevor raised his eyebrows, as if he'd never heard of such a thing.

"Not if I can help it." A bell dinged, alerting them to the arrival of their car. "And my office downtown is on the seventh floor."

"You must have fantastic glutes."

"Maybe you'll find out," Marc said under his breath once Trevor had walked into the vacant car ahead of him.

Trevor leaned against the back wall and dropped his bag to the floor, his eyes inviting, his smile seductive, and Marc didn't wait for the elevator doors to shut. Two quick steps brought him into Trevor's space, close enough to feel the soft gusts of breath fanning his cheek.

"Hold on!" someone shouted, and then a hand snaked between the closing doors, forcing them back open, and a frazzled-looking woman pushed inside. Marc managed to suppress a groan and stepped back to press number five on the keypad. He met Trevor's eyes and grinned, receiving a roll of the eyes and subtle head shake in return.

The woman pressed floor number nine—*figures*—and then shook the snow off her coat.

"Phew! What a night, huh?"

Marc couldn't agree more. This was going to be one long elevator ride.

CHAPTER SIX

*M*arc sat on the edge of the bed and blindly flipped through the channels on the TV, his body thrumming with nervous anticipation. All he could hear was the sound of the shower roaring in his ears like a tidal wave. An imaginary movie played in his mind, featuring one very naked Trevor, water running down his tall, lanky frame. Soap suds sliding lazily over muscle and skin and hair. Oh, how he hoped Trevor had hair on his chest and didn't manscape anywhere. Nothing turned him on more than playing with the soft pelt covering a man's chest, burying his nose in crinkly musk-scented pubic hair . . .

And what he wouldn't give to be that bar of soap right now, licking and tasting every glorious dip and swell, nook and cranny with his tongue.

A groan rolled up his throat, and he opened the front of his slacks, spreading his legs wide. Relief from the pressure of being constricted quickly led to a throbbing need for release. It had been a long time since he'd gone out with the intention of hooking up, and it'd been a good two years since his attempt at a relationship with Tony. He hadn't realized how much he needed a night like this, a night of simple human interaction at its most basic and primal. A brief interlude from his attempts to become the most successful son any mother could hope for.

The sound of running water stopped, metal screeched on metal, the shower curtain probably being pulled back. A moment of silence before the bathroom door swung open. Trevor stood there, steam dancing behind him, wearing only a towel slung loosely around his trim waist. There was a cream-colored bandage around Trevor's left biceps, but Marc's attention was drawn back to the towel like a moth to a flame. The ends didn't quite meet, exposing a meaty upper thigh and coming dangerously close to revealing an enticing bulge. A dusting of dark hair covered Trevor's chest. Not too thick, just a nice layering over well-defined pecs and abs, and a clear treasure trail leading down beneath the towel. Marc's fingers twitched with the need to touch.

"Sorry." Trevor's voice sounded rough and anything but apologetic. "I forgot to take a change of clothes into the bathroom with me." But he made no move to get dressed, as steam continued to drift out from behind him and water droplets trickled down his shoulders and chest, glittering like diamonds.

Marc nodded. Between the beautiful nearly naked man in his room and that sultry voice, there wasn't much blood left in his brain for optimum functioning.

He stared at Trevor. Trevor stared back. The electricity Marc had felt earlier crackled between them again, pricking at his skin and sending a flood of goose bumps over his arms. He swallowed and pushed the heel of his hand against his erection, seeking friction and drawing Trevor's gaze. When their eyes reconnected, Trevor licked his lips.

That was all the invitation Marc needed. He rose from the bed and crossed the short distance, slow and deliberate. Trevor didn't move a muscle, other than to lift one side of his mouth until it formed the sexiest, most wicked grin Marc had ever seen.

He stopped a foot shy of Trevor and reached out with one hand, then paused, letting his fingertips hover just over the surface of Trevor's belly. Close enough to feel the heat radiating from his moist flesh, to feel the rousing tingle of desire jump the slim space between them like a living thing, enticing him, captivating him.

He raised his eyes to meet Trevor's heavy-hooded blues. "Yes?"

"Yes." His hoarse whisper resonated with a need that echoed Marc's. "Please."

Oh, where to begin? All that sleek, hot, shower-damp skin . . .

Marc touched his index and middle fingertips to the ledge of an abdominal muscle just above Trevor's navel. Trevor's sharp intake of breath sent a jolt of desire skittering through Marc. He traced the shape before flattening his palm over the firm muscle, moving slowly upward, following curves and contours until his hand rested on the flat plane of Trevor's left pectoral. He brought his other hand up to Trevor's chest and slid them both over Trevor's collarbone, along the corded muscles of his neck, and then cupped his face.

Trevor trembled, his breath coming quicker, shallower, but otherwise he remained still. He let Marc explore as he wanted, waiting, maybe to see what Marc would do or what their roles would be. Marc didn't care. All he knew with any certainty was that he wanted Trevor. The how didn't matter.

He pulled Trevor to him, and their lips met for the first time. The sparks that had been zapping between them all night exploded bright and brilliant. There was none of that awkward first-kiss business Marc had experienced before. With Trevor only an inch or two taller than him, there was no issue of them angling the same way at the same time and bumping noses, no clashing of teeth or mouths not quite in sync. Not too much lip, or too much tongue, or too much saliva . . . It was as if their lips, their mouths, had been created solely for the other. A perfect fit.

When Trevor opened for him and their tongues tangled, Marc realized he'd been wandering alone in the desert on the verge of dehydration until this moment, and this man was his oasis.

What the hell?

He broke the kiss with a gasp, his breath rapid in its wake. The power of it was too overwhelming, yet he immediately wanted to dive back in. Was that all it took? Just one kiss and he was a goner? He was a damn lawyer! Logical and analytical and very left-brained. He didn't believe in things like love at first sight. Lust at first sight, absolutely. But hell, he couldn't deny the connection he'd felt since the moment he made eye contact with Trevor. Couldn't deny he currently felt something a little more than a commanding appetite for sex going on here. Lust had never left him waxing poetic about a kiss before.

"Top or bottom?" Marc asked, refocusing on the man before him and leaning down slightly to suck a hard nipple into his mouth, rolling his tongue around it.

"Verse," Trevor rasped. "But tonight, total bottom. *Please.*"

Oh God. Marc shivered. "Yes." His voice was barely audible, but going by the flare in the blue depths of those intense eyes, Trevor had heard him loud and clear.

Trevor leaned in and reclaimed Marc's mouth in a kiss more confident and demanding than the first, and though it had only been mere seconds, Marc had already been missing Trevor's taste. He gave himself up to it, letting Trevor lead him at will.

Panting filled the air, gasps for breath stolen between kisses Marc didn't want to stop. And it seemed, neither did Trevor. All the while Trevor quickly worked to remove Marc's shirt, but at the same time he was going excruciatingly slow. Trevor pushed the fabric off his shoulders, then ducked his head to trap a nipple between his teeth, giving a teasing tug before sucking it into his mouth as though his life depended on it. Marc groaned and closed his eyes. Yes, this was what he wanted, what he'd been missing for too long now—the need to be desired, wanted.

He ran a hand through Trevor's hair, soft and long enough to grip a fistful of, which he did. With his other hand, he yanked the towel from Trevor's waist, and his fully erect, wanting cock bobbed between them. Resting his forehead on Trevor's shoulder, Marc licked his lips, watching himself wrap his hand around the beautiful length. Hot, silken skin slid along the firm column of flesh in his grip. Trevor shook and moaned over Marc's nipple, hands moving south and thumbs tucking into the waistband of Marc's briefs, pushing them until both his underwear and slacks fell away and pooled on the ground at his feet.

Trevor leaned back to look down, and Marc's skin pebbled. "Good God, you're gorgeous."

Heat once again rose in Marc's face. How he could still be nervous at this point, with the two of them standing face-to-face stark naked, he didn't know. They were just two men making the most of an unforeseen situation. Nothing more. Yet, somewhere deep inside was a growing need to make sure it would be good for the both of them.

He shook his head and quickly dropped to his knees. Hopefully Trevor hadn't noticed the flush of red that had surely spread over his cheeks. He licked his lips and then wrapped them around Trevor's hard length. His eyes closed as he reveled in the bittersweet taste, the solid feel, and again, that oddly strong desire to give this man everything he had, to make this the best, most memorable experience of Trevor's life, hit him. Why it mattered so much just then wasn't something he had any capacity to analyze, but he would. Later. Maybe. But for now, his only focus, his only purpose, was Trevor's pleasure.

Trevor cradled Marc's head firmly but without force or control, just assurance and encouragement, and slowly began to rock his hips. Marc took him as deep as he could, but he had a bad gag reflex, so he used his hand as an extension of his mouth.

"Oh yeah." Trevor's low, rumbling voice drew Marc's attention, and he raised his eyes. Their stares connected, locked. Whatever Trevor saw there caused his breath to catch. "Fuuuuuuuuuuck." The word drew out on a growl.

A swell of pride filled Marc's chest at the clear effect he was having on Trevor. The strange nerves that had plagued him since first meeting Trevor vanished in that moment. He knew how to do this—was damn good at this, in fact—and he would give his all.

Spurred on by Trevor's rough noises and body signals, Marc began giving head in earnest, making sure to use every single trick he had in his arsenal. That Trevor was so clearly loving what Marc was doing made him want to bring the man off right away. But at the same time, he wanted to savor and prolong the pleasure. His jaw started to ache and his eyes began to water, but he was not letting go of that beautiful piece of man in his mouth.

"St-stop." Trevor groaned, a pained edge to his voice. "Stop. I don't want to come until you're inside me."

Jesus. Marc let go, sat back on his heels, and looked up. Trevor smiled and ran the pad of a finger over Marc's open mouth like a caress. "Your lips are swollen."

Marc smiled before flicking his tongue out to swirl around the long digit, and then closed his lips over it and sucked it to the base, his cheeks hollowing.

"Holy hell." A tremor racked Trevor's body. "That alone is enough to make me lose my load." He slowly retrieved his finger, then pulled Marc to his feet, fusing their mouths together in an impassioned kiss while guiding them toward the bed.

Trevor pulled back abruptly. "Please say you have condoms?"

"God, I hope so." Because the last thing he wanted to do was get dressed and leave this room for any reason. Even for that. Well, okay. Maybe he would for that, but he still didn't want to. He wanted to spend every possible moment with Trevor until the morning came and the roads were cleared.

He frowned. What the hell was going on with him tonight? It wasn't like he'd never had a fling before. Maybe the fact that it'd been so long since he'd felt connected to another man, coupled with Kate's worry about him missing out on life, was throwing him off. Pushing the weirdness away, he focused on the task at hand. He riffled through his gym bag, and fortunately, found two foil packets in the side panel, along with some lube. He held them up. "All set."

Trevor sat down and shimmied himself up the bed until he was dead center. Marc couldn't wait to slide his tongue all over that honeyed skin . . .

The bandage on Trevor's arm caught his attention again, but just as he was about to ask what had happened, Trevor spread his legs and ran his tongue over his lips, slow and sensual. Marc groaned. He didn't need to know anything. Just feel.

He climbed onto the bed, straddling Trevor, who was watching intently. Marc's balls brushed Trevor's abdomen, the fine hairs tickling his sac, and a rush of anticipation trembled in his stomach. He lowered himself, pressing their groins together, and moaned at the heavenly pressure. Marc didn't really need to do anything more than just lie there, their bodies molded together like two pieces of a puzzle. Such simple human contact, but that alone would be enough to see him through the night, before the new day spit him back out into his solitary world.

Trevor slipped a hand around the back of Marc's neck, his fingers threading through the short hair. "Sable."

Marc frowned. "What?"

"The color of your hair." Trevor met Marc's gaze, and that sexy grin of his sent all kinds of enticing vibrations through Marc. "Rich, almost . . . mahogany. Gold and burnt umber when the light catches it. Like sunshine."

Marc laughed, even as the words sent a wave of warmth through his chest. "It's just brown hair."

"There's no such thing as 'just brown.'" Trevor raised his other hand and ran his fingers up the side of Marc's neck, along his jaw and the line of his cheekbone, his gaze following the tactile exploration. "I want to paint you."

Marc swallowed against a tightening throat. "I thought you wanted to fuck me?" His voice was rough, constrained sounding, but he knew Trevor would mistake it for arousal rather than what it really was: his own compelling drive to create, to awaken that long-buried part of himself. A part he didn't think could ever find its way to the surface again but that he still mourned in the silent hours.

"No, I want *you* to fuck *me*." Trevor smiled and tugged at Marc's lower lip with a finger. Marc caught it with his teeth, teasing the tip with his tongue. "And *then* I'm going to paint you."

Marc didn't see how that was going to happen since they wouldn't be seeing each other again after tonight. Something pinched deep in his chest at that, but he ignored it. He pushed all thoughts of gorgeous artists and painting and dead dreams aside, and he leaned down to lose himself in the man underneath him. The kiss was slow and consuming and not at all timid. There was a determined force to it, a sense that they were skimming the fringes of control, and it was exactly what Marc needed.

He slipped his tongue inside to tango with Trevor's, reveling in the intensity and desire that rolled off their bodies in thick waves, coating his skin to the point where he could probably orgasm from that alone. He was so absorbed in the kiss he hadn't noticed when Trevor had pushed his hand between their bodies, forcing Marc to lift his hips, until a firm, warm grip closed around his length. A thrill skittered up his spine, and he moaned into Trevor's mouth.

Marc rocked leisurely into his hand at first, keeping pace with the slow dance of their mouths and tongues. And then urgency replaced the languid discovery of this man he'd chosen to spend his night with, share his body with. He had to touch everywhere at once. He couldn't *not*. His hand mussed Trevor's soft, shoulder-length hair, caressed his face and his neck, followed the length of his torso to his hip and flank, and tucked underneath to cup a solid, flexing butt cheek in his palm. He never once broke the kiss that had morphed from dancing foreplay into a seductive duel.

Trevor released Marc's cock, much to his dismay, and pushed against his shoulders, forcing him up, ending the kiss that Marc didn't think he'd ever get enough of. Trevor's breath gusted over Marc's chin in rapid bursts as his own ruffled strands of hair hung in Trevor's eyes. Air caught in Marc's lungs at the heated look in those blue oceans as they gazed up at him.

He reached for the packets he'd dropped on the bed beside them, and Trevor grinned before rolling onto his stomach. He lifted his hips and rubbed his ass against Marc's groin, sending sparks shooting off in every direction and causing a rough laugh to bubble up from his chest. "Tease."

He could honestly say he'd never made a sound like that in all his life, but at that moment, he was too far gone for embarrassment to make any kind of headway. Especially when Trevor went and spread his legs wider.

"Only if I don't follow through," Trevor countered, glancing over his shoulder with a sly glint in his eyes.

Marc settled between those long, toned limbs, his gaze falling on a perfectly round, muscular bottom. Each cheek fit perfectly in his open palms as he squeezed and caressed, spread and kneaded, his thumbs dipping into the crease between and following it down to the only place he wanted to be just then. Trevor pushed and rocked into his touch, silently pleading for more. A plea Marc was definitely not going to let go unanswered.

The sound of tearing foil ratcheted up Trevor's anticipation, and a second later, he flinched as cold liquid dripped onto his overheated skin.

"You have a beautiful ass," Marc said softly, the praise in his voice causing a pleasant flutter in Trevor's chest. He couldn't manage more than a rumbling "Mmm" in response. His focus was fully on Marc as he worked the lube into all the right places—warming, massaging, teasing, opening.

He'd had no reservations about going up to Marc's room, knowing full well where it would lead, but he'd not intended on bottoming. Not after so many years of nearly nonexistent sexual interest. Especially not with someone he'd never see again. But by the time they'd made their way to the room, his every nerve had been on fire. He'd wanted Marc, for sure. When he'd stepped out of the bathroom after his shower and seen the raw look of desire in Marc's eyes—the way he had asked permission to touch him, and then done so with such reverence—everything had changed. If this was going to be his last winter, and this man was his last chance to fully experience the human connection at its most primal, then he was damned well going to make the most of it.

So he gave himself up to Marc's sure hands, letting this handsome, switch-flipping stranger work him into a boneless state of euphoria. He dropped his head into the crook of his right elbow, bowing his back, opening himself further for Marc to do to him as he pleased. And so far, it was well more than *pleasing*.

"Ready for me?" Clear arousal gave a rough, shiver-inducing sharpness to Marc's voice.

"Yes. So much yes."

Another tear of foil, the sound amplified by the desire strumming through his veins, pressure at his hole. Excitement trembled over his skin as Marc slowly entered him. His entire world narrowed to that beautiful crash of their meeting bodies. The glorious burning stretch as he teetered on the cliff of pleasure-pain. The reverent push-pull as Marc inched deeper and deeper, asking Trevor's body to accept him. And he did.

Hot and hard, Marc filled him. His cock dragged over Trevor's prostate, forcing a moan up Trevor's throat and Marc's body to tremble. He pushed steadily until he was fully seated inside, somehow reaching beyond what Trevor ever could have thought possible.

Trevor squeezed around the man buried inside him, drawing a growling gasp from Marc. One hand gripped and kneaded his butt cheeks while the other fisted his balls, rolling them, caressing them. "Now," he ground out, his voice muffled in the cocoon of his arm. He turned his head, and their eyes locked. "Come on, Marc. Fuck me like you own me."

Trevor's breath caught on the flare of desire that lit Marc's deep-green irises.

Holy . . . yeah. Marc was a vision of awe-inspiring virility.

"Jesus . . ." Marc said, frozen still, as if his entire body was holding its breath. In that suspended pause, bodies joined, pulses pounding as one, Trevor didn't think it was possible they could ever separate again. At least not until hot breath gusted over his sensitive back, and Marc did as Trevor had bid, easing almost all the way out until just the head of his cock teased the ring of Trevor's hole. He held there for a second, as if they were both taking that last gulp of oxygen before jumping off the cliff into a waiting lake below, and slammed back in. Deep. Mind-blowingly deep.

"Yes!" Trevor shouted, dropping his head down and digging his elbows into the mattress to brace himself.

Marc began pumping a hard rhythm, thrusts angled just right to hit Trevor's prostate on every stroke. His senses acutely tuned in to the wordless yet articulate language of their bodies. With each perfect drive of his cock, Marc freed Trevor from the stresses and burdens of his life. Out, in. Gone was the worry of his failing kidneys. Out, in. Gone was the bleak outlook of never finding a transplant. Out, in. Gone was the loss of dreams and hope. Out, in. Only this moment, this man. Out, in. Living breathing loving . . .

This was what he'd so desperately needed without even realizing it. To be taken, owned, desired, reminded that he was still alive—fully and completely. But then Marc pulled out all the way, leaving him empty and scrabbling to get that escape back. He growled, the vibration grating over his vocal chords.

"Roll over," Marc rasped, hands on his hips gently guiding him. "I want to see your face when you lose it."

Trevor rolled to the right, flipping over, and Marc leaned down to kiss him, mouth sliding over his, tongues twining with desperate need. Marc lowered his body, pressing their cocks between their bellies, the two of them rocking together.

"Fuck, you're so hot," Trevor gasped between kisses. "But I need . . ."

. . . *you to take me away. Make me forget. Show me I'm whole and healthy and vibrant like you.*

". . . Fuck me." He dug his fingers into Marc's shoulders, his back, his ass. "Fuck me."

"Shit." Marc plundered his mouth, sucking on his tongue, kissing him deep and with complete abandon. "I have never met anyone like you."

"*Marc.*"

"Yes."

One more brain-stalling kiss, and then Marc leaned back, lifting Trevor's legs and settling them over his shoulders. Trevor's eyelids fluttered, and a moaning growl tore from his raw throat as Marc gripped his thighs and pushed back inside, forcing worry and depression and fatigue to surrender. His every nerve sang in relief.

"Look at me," Marc demanded.

He obeyed. Marc's gaze, completely unguarded by passion, locked on his as he stared at Trevor like he was the only thing in the world that mattered. A tiny pang of regret dared to threaten the moment, but he aggressively shoved it away. Only right now mattered. The play of the muscles of Marc's face as he pumped in and out mattered. The deep flush that spread over his chest, up his neck, into his cheeks with the effort of their lovemaking mattered. Dark hair, damp with sweat, and the sheen on olive skin mattered.

"Damn, you're a beautiful man," Marc said, with something like awe in his voice. Or maybe Trevor just imagined that.

Marc held one of Trevor's thighs to his chest and caressed Trevor's chest and stomach with his other hand, sliding lower and lower until he clasped Trevor's cock.

"Yesss." Trevor moaned and placed his hand over Marc's, and together they brought him closer and closer to the edge. Their mingled breaths came faster, louder, rougher.

"Come." Marc's voice was ragged and strained. "Come for me."

"Oh . . . Fuck . . . Marc . . ." Trevor threw his head back, squeezed his eyes shut, and thick cum splattered his abdomen in fierce pulses, the rush of his orgasm powerful enough to gray his vision and rack his whole body with delightful tremors. He tightened his inner muscles, squeezing around the hard cock lodged deep inside him, urging Marc to join his release.

Marc dropped forward, arms braced on either side of Trevor, and pounded into him, hard and fast. Sweat dripped off his nose, and harsh pants blew against Trevor's face before Marc's body tensed. His rhythm jerked, and then he held still. He was so rooted that Trevor could feel Marc's cock throbbing inside him, and for a second, he wondered how it would feel if there were nothing between them.

Marc collapsed on top of him, the weight a welcome blanket rather than an uncomfortable crush. Trevor snaked a hand around the back of Marc's neck and claimed his mouth in a heated kiss. Not breaking their kiss, Marc eased himself out of Trevor's body while covering it at the same time. And Trevor found himself thinking, as spent and exhausted as he was, he didn't want this night to end.

Marc slowed the kiss; it became addicting, languid, and somehow more powerful than all the ones previous. Somehow it seemed to mean more, as though Marc was saying something Trevor should be able to understand. Or most likely, he was simply lost in an incredible postorgasmic haze, and his mind really had been blown.

Because that's what this was. One random night of mind-blowing sex. A brief escape from his inevitable end.

Marc pulled his lips away gently and stared down at Trevor, eyes unreadable.

"I feel you thinking, counselor," Trevor teased, because that look made him feel exposed and vulnerable in a way he couldn't allow. Not now. Not ever.

Marc smiled, and whatever Trevor thought he'd seen in the man's gaze was gone. Thankfully. He rolled them to their sides, pulled the blankets over them, and wrapped Marc in his arms, their faces barely an inch apart.

"I'm thinking this was some sort of fortunate blizzard," Marc said.

Trevor smiled against the nervous twinge in his chest. "That's kind of philosophical for a lawyer."

Marc nudged him with his knee, the side of his mouth crooked up. "Your artsy-fartsy ways must be contagious."

CHAPTER SEVEN

revor cracked an eye open and focused on the neon-green glow from the clock radio on the bedside table. It was not quite 5 a.m. He'd slept all of four hours before his internal alarm nudged him out of the much-needed slumber. Or maybe that was his bladder insisting he get up right now. The added pressure of an arm draped over his waist only forced the issue.

He gently crawled out from under Marc, careful not to wake him, and stumbled blindly toward the bathroom. After relieving himself, he unwrapped the gauze bandage on his biceps and checked the fistula grafted to a vein in his arm. If there'd been any serious damage to it he'd have known immediately, but in the throes of passion, a minor impact could still damage it. Which would cause a problem for his dialysis treatments and might even mean surgery for a new one. Satisfied it was okay, he loosely rewrapped his arm. He didn't need the gauze for anything other than his own vanity, hiding the fistula so he didn't have to explain to Marc what it was.

He glanced at himself in the mirror. How could he look so . . . normal, yet be so sick that he was literally knocking on death's door? Scowling, he slapped the light switch off.

Back in the room, he crept to the window and pulled the curtains back a few inches. Snow was still falling in thick lazy flakes, burying the world in blue-cast white. If it didn't stop soon, there'd be no getting a flight out today, either.

He turned, and the sigh that had begun a slow exhale up his throat caught midway. A spear of light from the parking lot lights fell over Marc's bare torso, giving him an ethereal radiance. He'd turned over after Trevor had left the bed and was now facing the window. The sheets were pushed down to his hip, one hand tucked under his head, the other open flat on the now-empty space where Trevor had been.

Trevor pushed the curtains back a little farther, letting more light spill over Marc's body, careful to keep it from hitting his eyes and waking him. Trevor's fingers twitched at his side, and that familiar urge to capture the image before him welled up inside. He tiptoed to his bag and quietly pulled out a sketch pad and a set of graphite pencils. Then he dragged one of the table chairs in front of the window. He sat down and opened his book to a fresh page.

The light wasn't great for drawing, but it was enough. He studied Marc, following the line of his shoulder to the dip between his rib cage and hip bone, along the dark shadows playing across his relaxed muscles and the folds of the sheet where it lay over his body, hiding what Trevor remembered was a beautiful, thick cock. The dull ache in his body reminded him how good it had been too. And surprised him. He hadn't experienced arousal like this in years, an unfortunate side effect of his treatments. But the man sleeping soundly five feet away from him had managed to reignite his system with a single glance.

A smile tugged at the corners of his mouth. Every second had been worth it. He couldn't remember the last time he'd felt so alive, so unburdened from facing and fighting his inevitable death. It was as if Marc somehow knew and had made sure that what they'd done last night wasn't just two strangers having sex. It was Marc making love to him.

A shiver slid up his spine and over his shoulders, and he shook the thoughts away. Fantasizing wasn't going to change anything. But Marc was gorgeous, and had given him a reprieve from his constant battle. He could paint the man. He *needed* to.

Settling comfortably into the chair, he resumed his study of Marc. Muscular legs and an incredible ass from all the stair-climbing the man did remained hidden underneath the off-white sheet. One of Marc's knees was bent forward, his other leg stretched behind. His foot twitched. Trevor rose and walked over to the bed, carefully rearranging the blankets to expose Marc's foot and leg to midthigh. He stood back for a moment, tilted his head to the side, and then stepped forward to once more arrange the sheets to his liking—smoothing a fold here, puffing up a fold there, revealing a little more skin. Just a touch more light on the end of the bed . . . He opened the left curtain another inch, then one more, and there . . . *Perfect.*

Trevor sat back down and started the first strokes of his sketch. He'd always found drawing someone, painting them, to be an extremely intimate experience. Through that experience he discovered the hearts and souls of the people he brought to life on paper or canvas—or whatever surface happened to be handy when the urge struck—without touching or even speaking to them. It was his personal study of humanity through expression of the physical form, and it had become his signature in the art world. His ability to pull raw emotion out of a two-dimensional image was what had broken him out onto the main stage and kept him there.

But his current muse . . . There was more to him than met the eye, something hidden in his depths that Trevor *had* to coax out. It was behind a shadow that drifted over deep-green eyes, the note of longing in his sonorous voice when he'd asked about Trevor's art, a twitch and tilt of his head followed by a shy hint of a smile on soft lips that belied his outward confidence, and the flush of pink that sometimes colored his sharp cheekbones. The man was successful, affluent, gorgeous. On the surface he seemed to have it all. But a sense of loss or solitude lurked behind the strong, self-assured front. Trevor got the sense that even in sleep Marc had a story to tell, something he was afraid of. Whatever his story was, it bubbled so close to the surface that it seemed Marc was still guarding it as he dreamed.

Awareness tiptoed around the edges of Marc's consciousness, and a strange sense of being watched tagged along with it. Without moving or opening his eyes, he tried to take stock of his surroundings. The bed didn't feel like his, and the sheets smelled of industrial detergent and sex. There was a low hum, and a faint scratching against the peaceful stillness in the air. He wasn't at home. He was in a hotel room . . . with a handsome man. They'd had fantastic sex.

And now he was in that bed alone, although he wasn't the only one in the room.

He lifted an eyelid just enough to see an out-of-focus Trevor sitting in front of the window, low light from outside casting a soft glow around his shoulders. Outside, snow continued to dot the dark-gray skies behind him. Trevor's head was down, the ankle of one leg resting across the knee of the other, and his attention focused on the sketchbook that leaned against the easel his leg created. His hand moved across the page in deliberate strokes, almost affectionate in the way it danced over its surface. Marc watched, unable to look away or move, and that secreted part of his soul cried.

Trevor's hand paused its hypnotic flow, breaking his trance, and he glanced up. Marc's lungs froze mid-inhale, afraid to give any sign that he'd awoken and disturb an artist in his element. By Trevor's intense stare aimed at the foot of the bed, Marc didn't have anything to worry about. Except a sudden urge to wiggle his exposed toes.

Trevor returned his attention to the sketchbook, a lock of thick hair falling over his forehead. How had their paths never crossed before now? With Trevor living in Nederland, there were less than twenty miles between them. But then, with work such a heavy demand on his time, Marc rarely spent any time in Boulder simply enjoying what it had to offer. He was always either in the office or at home.

Besides, Trevor undoubtedly traveled the art circles that Marc had avoided most of his life. Not because he didn't appreciate art but because pursing it wouldn't make his mother proud. He'd never fully let go of that lost dream though. The house he'd purchased had spoken to the buried part of himself that refused to die, even after being starved for decades. He'd gone so far as to dedicate a room as an art studio where he could revisit his first passion . . . and then never stepped inside it again.

"I wanted to be an artist," Marc blurted, catching himself off guard. Heat infused his cheeks at having spoken at all, let alone given voice to his forgotten dream.

Trevor startled, his hand jerking on the page, and a trickle of guilt snaked into Marc's chest. "Sorry, I didn't mean to interrupt."

Or say anything at all. Especially that.

Trevor shook his head, the near-silhouette of his smile soft. He closed the sketchbook and stood, placing it and a pencil kit back in his travel bag before returning to the bed and stretching out beside Marc.

"Yeah?" Trevor rose up to lean on his elbow, one hand caressing Marc's chest and abs in lazy figure eights.

Marc glanced up at him, that stare gently prompting him to continue, telling him that Trevor somehow understood and that Marc would be safe revealing his deepest secrets, if he chose to, to a stranger he'd never see again. Did that make it easier or harder? Did spilling secrets in the dark count? He tore his gaze away with effort and looked out the window, not really seeing anything beyond it.

Marc shrugged. "Just idealistic dreams of youth."

"I doubt that."

Marc met Trevor's gaze again, those bright-blue eyes offering encouragement. It was the first time he'd given voice to a lost dream, and now he wasn't so sure where to go from there. The things he did, like setting up the room he never ventured inside, didn't require more than a disconnected, peripheral-type of thinking. Art was always in the back of his mind but never truly brought into the light. Like the shadow of movement out of the corner of an eye, but no matter how fast you turn your head to catch it, nothing's there.

"I used to love painting." He paused, swallowing back a sudden tightness in his throat. "I was actually pretty good at it, according to my teachers. My mother would say, 'That's nice, honey,' and occasionally stick one of my projects on the fridge. But it wasn't long before I noticed my two brothers were receiving more enthusiastic praise and support for their sports and academic achievements. She never outright discouraged me, but more and more I came to realize she wasn't quite as proud of me."

Marc huffed a halfhearted laugh. "She didn't even make it to my first art exhibit because one of my brothers had soccer practice that day. Not even a game, just a regular, everyday practice."

"How old were you?" Trevor's voice was soft and held a note of empathy, but thankfully not pity.

"Fourteen. That was my one and only art show. I loved art. It was like . . . breathing." He searched Trevor's eyes, which looked steel gray in the dim light, and in that moment felt like he'd found a kindred spirit. Would his life have been different if he'd met someone like

Trevor twenty years ago? Maybe, maybe not, but one thing he did know: there was no point in wasting time on what-ifs.

"But the need to make my mother proud of me was stronger, so I gave my paints and canvases away and focused on academics. I think I saw her first genuinely smile at me when I told her I'd decided to be a lawyer. It seemed like I'd finally won her approval." He took a deep breath. All these years and the memory still hadn't lost its painful bite. "And then my youngest brother outed me when I was sixteen."

Marc fell silent, his mind traveling back in time to that day, and his stomach did a nauseating flop. They'd been eating dinner—Marc, his mother, and his brothers, Rick and Andy. Marc hadn't known at the time, but Andy had seen him kissing his first boyfriend. As soon as the words had left Andy's lips, the temperature had dropped in the room, and a chill had crawled up his spine. His mother had just stared at him, her expression completely blank.

"Is that true?" she'd asked in a flat voice. All Marc could do was nod at her, barely making eye contact, and then he glared at his brother, who'd smirked back. The moment had stretched on in uncomfortable silence until finally his mother said, "I see." And that was it.

Trevor stopped trailing his fingers along Marc's skin when he didn't continue. "Please don't tell me your parents kicked you out."

Marc shook his head. "No. Though I sometimes think that would have been better. My mother just shut me out, instead. She didn't talk to me unless she had to. Nothing I ever did after that night was good enough. It was like I was a ghost—invisible in plain sight. And the day I turned eighteen she said I was an adult now and it was time to move out."

"What about your dad?"

"Absentee. They divorced when I was twelve, and he was too busy working and traveling to be a full-time father."

"I'm sorry."

Marc shrugged. "It was what it was. Could have been a whole lot worse."

Silence fell between them as that same desperate, crushing feeling sucked him back into its depths, trying to swallow him whole like they had all those years ago.

"How are things now?" Trevor's touch coasted down his arm, finding Marc's hand and twining their fingers together. The gesture pulled him back to the present. "She must be proud of how successful you've become?"

Marc shook his head slowly, giving the hand holding his a thankful squeeze. "I haven't talked to her in almost ten years. Not even a birthday or Christmas card."

Trevor was quiet for a second, and the broken hum of the room's heater seemed too loud for the otherwise-still night. "What about your brothers? How many do you have?"

"Two. Both younger. Rick, the middle son, accepted me. He was my best friend, tried to encourage me to paint again. But then he went and joined the Army." A lump swelled in his throat, preventing him from speaking for a moment. "He . . . he never made it back home."

"I'm so sorry, Marc," Trevor said, his voice soft as it mirrored the sense of loss that rose with a vengeance in Marc's chest. It had been years since Rick had been killed, but the pain never lessened.

"And then there's Andy . . ." Marc slid his hand out of Trevor's, the gesture suddenly too intimate now, and looked over Trevor's shoulder at the still-falling snow beyond the window. "The last thing he wanted was a faggot brother. I have no idea where he is now or what he's done with his life. I'm sure whatever it is, our mother is proud of him." Marc snapped his mouth shut, taken aback by the venom in his own words, and closed his eyes. He didn't want to see anything in Trevor's gaze that might add to his failure to measure up.

And why was he telling all of this to a man he'd just met? He'd never spoken aloud about his past or dreams to anyone, but then, he hadn't really thought about what he'd been doing in a long time. Making his mother proud of him had become his sole driving force for so long that there really wasn't room in his life for anything else.

"And you never went back to your art?"

"I'm . . . not ready yet."

"Art never really leaves your soul," Trevor said. "What's stopping you from picking up the brushes again?"

Marc sighed and rolled onto his back, lacing his fingers over his stomach as he stared at the dark ceiling. He was done with this conversation. Didn't know why he'd even brought it up in the first place. All it did was bring his mood down. "I don't have time for anything but work right now."

Trevor was silent for a long moment, and the air around them grew heavy, as if the pressure in the room was dropping. The heater fan kicked in again, a low and steady hum underscoring the tone of the atmosphere.

"Take it from me," Trevor said, his voice sounding distant and flat, something close to regret riding the underside of it. He mimicked Marc and rolled to his back, folding his hands over his stomach. "All we have is right now, so live it, as my mom says. You have to make the time for the things that matter most."

"Right now that's making partner at the firm," Marc said.

Trevor angled his head toward Marc, but he couldn't make out Trevor's expression. Trevor sucked in a shallow breath, and opened his mouth as if to speak but then nodded instead.

Marc got the distinct and uncomfortable feeling that he'd somehow disappointed Trevor too. Which was ridiculous. He'd just met the guy mere hours ago. Granted, he couldn't deny a crazy-strong connection, but that could be due to being stranded in the blizzard with a gorgeous and willing man. None of it mattered, anyway. He'd never see Trevor again after tonight, so why the hell should he care what the man thought?

"I'm curious," he said, hoping to shift the topic back to Trevor, when really, he should just roll over and go back to sleep. Tomorrow was going to be another long day digging himself out of the snow. "What were you drawing? If you don't mind my asking?"

Trevor turned onto his side, back to Marc, and pulled the covers to his chin. "Time."

CHAPTER EIGHT

The sun was shining through the hotel room window when Marc awoke a few hours later, his mind, body, and soul fully sated. He smiled at the man wrapped around him and wondered how a handful of hours could feel so significant. Trevor was a stranger, and yet he wasn't.

He glanced at the clock and the smile slowly slipped from his lips—twenty to nine. By now, the roads would probably be cleared enough to get traffic moving again, and this incredible night would soon be a mere memory. He found himself wishing they could be stranded just a bit longer. He caught himself. *No.* That was foolish, wishful thinking, and not like him at all. What he needed to do was get up and get moving, get his head back on work where it belonged.

"I hear you thinking again." Trevor's voice was rough from sleep, and the raw tenor sent a flush of arousal to Marc's groin. He gazed into the blue pair of sleepy yet still-mesmerizing eyes and decided real life could wait just a little bit longer.

"What do you say we make the most of this fine morning before hitting the road?" He slipped a hand between them, taking a firm but gentle hold of Trevor's semierect penis and coaxing it awake.

"I was going to say you wore me out last night, but . . ." A half chuckle, half moan escaped Trevor's throat, as if he were taken off guard by his arousal. "Seems you have the magic touch."

Marc smiled and shimmied closer so he could align their cocks and stroke them together. The slide of hot velvet skin in his palm, the moans of pleasure rumbling from Trevor's chest, sent a thrill through his nervous system. Trevor's hand joined his, both of them holding each other as one, pumping, squeezing, twisting. Marc's hips rocked into the heavenly grip of their own accord as he leaned forward and kissed Trevor. Mindless of lingering morning breath, he explored and tasted and savored the raw flavor of a man who could easily become an addiction. The thought should have been frightening, but instead only increased Marc's desire.

Trevor used his body and free hand to push Marc to his back, then broke their kiss and, with a sly twinkle in his eyes and a seductive grin stretching his lips, slunk down Marc's body, kissing as he went. A hand slid over the flat plane of his abdomen, into the crease of his thigh and groin, then under to cup and caress his balls. Marc spread his legs wider and lifted his hips to give Trevor more room to play. A finger teased behind his sac, to his hole, circling but not breaching, and the moan that rolled up his throat grated over his vocal chords like sandpaper. Trevor met his gaze, grin broadening, and then he dropped down and swallowed Marc's cock in one swift but sexy motion.

Marc's grating moan morphed into a growl loud enough to echo off the walls. All thought escaped as the wet heat engulfed his sensitive flesh, the teasing of a strong tongue, the glorious, glorious suction, the hint of teeth . . . Every blowjob before this paled in comparison, and a new bar was set for all those in the future. A thought flitted through the back of his mind, but he couldn't quite grasp hold of it. It seemed important that he work the thought out, but his balls began to tighten and the world focused sharply to that incredible point of connection where Trevor held him on the brink with his hands and mouth. As if Trevor knew exactly what he was doing to him and how far to push, he popped his mouth off Marc's dick and sucked one of his balls into his mouth while rolling the other in his hand. Every nerve ending sizzled and sparked.

"Ah, hell . . . Trev. Stop."

Trevor obeyed, but the glint in his eyes suggested he was only humoring him. Marc pushed him away before he could dive back down to finish what he'd started. The confusion and disappointment that cut across his features quickly morphed back into playful pleasure when Marc shifted around so they were lying feet to head.

His gaze tracked slowly up Trevor's body until their eyes met, and he waggled his eyebrows. "Now the boys can both party."

"Brilliant idea," Trevor teased, grabbing his own cock and tapping it gently against Marc's cheek. "No wonder you're such a successful lawyer."

Marc covered Trevor's hand with his, stilling his movements. "I do have a proven track record."

"Well, then." Trevor removed his hand and ran it through Marc's hair, cradling the back of his head. "Show me how—"

Trevor's words turned to senseless garble when Marc wasted no time wrapping his lips around the head of Trevor's cock, wanting to show him everything he could do. Trevor mirrored his actions, the slick heat of his mouth consuming Marc once again. He offered no mercy as he swiftly brought Marc back to the edge with his mouth and tongue, and this time, he gently pressed two long, agile fingers inside him. And that was it.

If Trevor hadn't already had him skirting on the brink, Marc would've been embarrassed by how quickly he came. A powerful, body-shaking orgasm blasted through him, seemingly with no intention of ending. His body jerked, and he heard the sound of his voice but any words were muffled beyond recognition by the stiff column of flesh filling his mouth. Trevor held him in that hot cavern until he was fully spent, then gently released him, while using his tongue to caress his now-extrasensitive skin.

"And the high-powered attorney is bested by an artis—"

Oh no, you don't. Marc slid a finger into his mouth, alongside Trevor's cock, slicked it up, and then pressed it into Trevor's beautiful hole. All before the man could finish his sentence. He sucked harder while he pushed deeper, searching out Trevor's prostate. Trevor gasped and thrust into Marc's mouth when he'd hit the spot, and then bittersweet liquid rolled down his tongue and the back of his throat. He took it all, every last drop Trevor gave him, savoring it, committing the flavor to memory.

Marc flopped over onto his back and Trevor did the same. Marc reached for Trevor's hand and laced their fingers together. Trevor squeezed once and tightened their hold.

Marc's lips curled into a smile, and then he chuckled. "You were saying something about besting?"

Trevor looked over at him, his eyes dopey in a just-got-sexed-brilliantly kind of way that made Marc's chest swell. *I did that.*

"We may need a retrial." Trevor's voice was hoarse, but the promise sent a cold spike through Marc's postorgasmic bliss. This was a random one-nighter, and he was a grown man, a logical man, who didn't fall in love at first sight. He certainly was not doing that now, but he couldn't deny there was something strong and tangible going on between them. Something he wanted a whole lot more of.

The soft smile fell from Trevor's lips, and a faint crease appeared in his forehead, as if an unpleasant thought had crossed his mind, and he jumped from the bed. "Come on," he said, the tone of his voice a lighthearted contrast to his expression. He held out his hand, beckoning Marc to join him. "Let's clean up."

"I really don't think I can get it up again that fast." Marc chuckled but let Trevor haul him from the bed anyway. He'd certainly give it his best effort.

Trevor raised an eyebrow. "Did I say anything about sex?"

"Leading me to the shower where we'll be all naked and wet, and not having steamy sex?" Marc teased. "That's just wrong."

"Hmm..." Trevor led him across the room and into the bathroom, still holding his hand. "Didn't someone just say something about not being able to get it up so soon?"

"Details." Marc watched the play of muscle on Trevor's back as he leaned in to turn the shower on—flexing, stretching, contracting—and Marc couldn't stop from reaching out to feel the muscle move under his palm.

"Yes, details," Trevor said. He turned to Marc and kissed him with playful promise while they waited for the water to warm up. "If I'm going to paint you, I'll need to study your form."

Heat exploded into Marc's groin. "Jesus Christ. That is the sexiest thing anyone has ever said to me."

"You're showering with the wrong people, then." A light flush colored Trevor's cheeks before he turned to step inside the shower stall, pulling Marc with him. He angled their position so Marc was under the spray, and reached around behind him for the soap, holding Marc's gaze the whole time. It wasn't until he'd begun to slowly soap up Marc's body that he finally let go of his hand, using both to spread the lather.

Marc stood still, watching Trevor as he almost lovingly went about making sure not an inch of Marc was left untended to. He kneeled down to scrub Marc's legs, his groin, his balls, his penis, which liked the attention enough to begin filling out. Trevor looked up to meet his gaze and smiled. The tenderness in those eyes hit him right under the breastbone, breaking open a piece of himself too-long denied. But the taste of joy was tinged with something else . . . like yearning or regret. He couldn't be sure of which.

He cupped Trevor's cheek and then slid a finger along the seam of his mouth. Trevor opened and sucked the finger inside. But it was more than the act that struck Marc in ways he hadn't expected; it was the care and reverence Trevor was showing him. As though Marc was someone who mattered.

Loneliness. That's what it was. That was the feeling tainting the joy and contentment he'd been feeling nearly from the moment Trevor had sat down at his table the night before. Trevor's company made the emptiness all the more apparent. How many years was it now that he'd spent the holidays alone? Even before his mom told him it was time for him to move out, Christmas had been something to dread rather than look forward to. This time of year only amplified his unworthiness and left him pining away the holiday until he could get back on a normal schedule at work.

"Hey." Trevor's voice drew him back to the here and now. "Where did you go?"

"I'm right here."

Trevor rose to his feet and held the soap out. "Good, 'cause now it's my turn."

"Turn around, Picasso," Marc teased.

Trevor raised his eyebrows before turning his back to Marc. "Ha-ha. I'm far better than that hack."

"Hmm . . ." Marc kissed the nape of Trevor's neck and then nipped, earning a subtle tremble and a moan. "I think you just pissed off every art major on the planet."

"What's art without a little controversy?" A hint of breathlessness in Trevor's voice made Marc smile.

"What, indeed."

Marc ran his hands along the solid planes of Trevor's back, grazing the dimples just above his gorgeous butt cheeks, and slid the back of his hand through the crack. Marc had only been teasing about having sex in the shower. Mostly. This right now, though, just caressing each other, relaxing under the steady flow of hot water . . . He couldn't imagine a better way to end this random encounter.

And he refused to analyze why that thought made him frown.

Trevor disconnected the call and sighed, dropping his phone on the table with a *thunk*.

"No luck?" Marc asked as he exited the bathroom, stark naked and rubbing his shower-damp hair with a towel, his olive skin heat flushed, and Trevor's mouth watered.

He licked his lips and shook his head, watching Marc cross the room and pull a pair of sweatpants from his gym bag. "The airport is still grounded, and there are apparently over four thousand people camping out on the floors there. No one is flying anywhere today, and with that many already trying to rebook flights home, even if the runways reopen tomorrow, chances are slim I'll get on one."

Marc paused with his pants halfway on, and the warmth in those deep eyes tugged at Trevor's heart. "And tomorrow is Christmas Day. I'm really sorry you'll miss spending it with your family."

"Thanks, but not much I can do about it," Trevor said, hoping his voice didn't sound as upset as he was. His last Christmas, and he wouldn't be with them.

"Except make the most of it with a certain handsome stranger?" Marc waggled his eyebrows, and Trevor had to laugh.

"Except that," he agreed. They had definitely made the most of it—more than once—and he had the dull but glorious ache in his backside to prove it. He could go for more. *No.* There wouldn't be more. *Ever.*

A serious expression stole over Marc's features as if he'd heard Trevor's thoughts. He took a deep breath and opened his mouth.

Whatever he'd been about to say stalled at the simultaneous knock at the door, call of "Room service," and chirp of a cell phone.

Trevor stood, watching Marc, who snapped his mouth shut and only nodded before breaking their intense eye lock to answer his phone.

Trevor retrieved their breakfast cart with a thank-you and a tip, and then went about laying out their meals on the table. Scrambled eggs with bacon, hash browns, toast, and coffee for Marc; egg whites, fresh fruit, and water for Trevor. He'd already taken his vitamins, iron supplement, and meds while Marc had been finishing up in the bathroom, not wanting to have to explain the daily concoction, but popped two protein binders with a sip of the water. If Marc saw, he'd likely just assume they were vitamins.

"I'm just over at a hotel off the turnpike. I'll be there as soon as I can," Marc said. Paused, then, "Thank you." He ended the call, frowning as he pulled a T-shirt over his head and sat at the table across from Trevor.

"Everything okay?" Trevor asked.

Marc nodded, the frown gone as though it had never been there. "They've cleared the road. I'd left my number on the windshield so I wouldn't get towed, but I can't wait too long." He raised an eyebrow at each of their plates and gave Trevor a pointed look. "On a diet?"

"Something like that," Trevor said, finding himself with the urge to frown, now, too. But what for? This had been a beautiful way to pass the time, nothing more. In another life though . . . Marc might have been the kind of man he'd want more with.

"I'm suddenly feeling like a glutton," Marc said.

"Nah. I like a man with a healthy appetite," Trevor said and then flushed when the unintended innuendo lit a spark in Marc's eyes and tugged his lips into a sexy grin.

"Can I give you a ride somewhere? Home?" Marc dug into his breakfast with gusto, pulling a surprised smile from Trevor. He'd always loved to watch a man with a hearty appetite eat. He couldn't say why, but maybe it came from his nights on family dinner duty when he was growing up. Seeing people he cared about enjoying something he'd created for them gave him a wonderful feeling. Cooking had become a passion, right along with his art. And some would call cooking an art form too. He certainly did.

"Thank you, but no," he said, fighting a sudden longing to cook for Marc. "Boulder Canyon is snowed in, and crews don't anticipate getting the road open today. Even if I get back to the shuttle stop where I left my car, I won't be able to get up the mountain. I'm stuck here until I can get a flight out."

The fork Marc had been raising to his mouth paused, and that serious, thoughtful expression Trevor had seen earlier resurfaced. "So you'll be spending your Christmas here? In a hotel, by yourself?"

Another wave of homesickness, ten times stronger than last night, flooded through Trevor's veins, but he smiled, refusing to let it show. "With a couple hundred other stranded travelers also missing Christmas with their families, I won't be alone."

Marc studied him for a long moment, breaking the stare just before Trevor had the urge to squirm. Damn. If that look was anything like what Marc shot at the opposing bench in court, no wonder he was as successful as he claimed.

"Do you have a big family? Are you close?" Marc asked, funneling that attention back to his breakfast. He lifted his gaze, and the faintest of blushes colored his cheeks. "I'm sorry. I don't mean to be nosy, but . . . it's only fair, since some strange force came over me last night and I spilled my guts." He grinned. "Must have been all that artsy mojo stuff you've got going on."

Trevor laughed. "'Artsy mojo'?"

Marc shrugged without looking up, embarrassed maybe.

Trevor popped a strawberry in his mouth, pausing for a moment to chew before he spoke. One thing he'd learned last night was that there was a big emptiness inside of Marc. He needed someone in his life who would support him one hundred ten percent, who would always be there for him. No matter what. As much as Trevor might want to try to be that person, it just wasn't in the cards for him. He would leave Marc, and soon, whether he wanted to or not.

"I was adopted as a baby," he finally answered, "by the best family I could have ever asked for."

Marc lifted his gaze and smiled. "Those are the stories I like to hear."

"I have to agree," Trevor said. "My mom wasn't able to have children of her own, and she hates that there are so many unwanted children out there. I've got three brothers and two sisters, and we're an ethnic bunch of misfits. Even my parents: Dad is white and Mom is Hispanic. Xavier and Olivia are both Hispanic and older than me; the youngest of the bunch are Adeline and Alex, Chinese and white respectively; and Isaac, who is the same age as me, is black. Isaac and I have a long-standing argument over which of us is actually the older brother. Sometimes I think he's the oldest of all of us, with the way he takes care of everyone, including Mom and Dad."

"Sounds like a tight-knit family," Marc said, and Trevor didn't miss the note of longing in his rich voice.

"We are, but much to Mom and Dad's dismay, we're all grown up now, and me, Xavier, and Olivia moved out of state. Adeline still lives with them, Isaac's only five minutes away, and Alex lives a little farther out, but still in Connecticut."

"So what brought you all the way out to Colorado?"

"The mountains." Trevor smiled. "They feed my artistic soul. I mean, my artsy mojo."

Marc chuckled and put his fork down, his plate spotless. A wistful light flashed through his forest-colored eyes. "Yeah," he said. Just a couple of feet separated them, yet his voice managed to sound distant. "I can see that."

CHAPTER NINE

After breakfast, Marc gathered his belongings and called a cab. Now that the turnpike was open again, it was too dangerous to walk across it to retrieve his car. Trevor went with him to the hotel registration desk so he could take over Marc's room for another day, and a nagging sense of apprehension snaked back into Marc's bones. He needed to get going so he could work on his new case, but some part of him was digging its heels in, not wanting to end this . . . thing. He stomped it down. With biker boots on his mental feet.

"I'm sorry," the front desk clerk said as she handed back Marc's credit card. "There's a waitlist for rooms, with so many people stuck, and your room was already rebooked."

"Oh," Marc said, not sure what to say, or that there was anything *to* say, and turned to Trevor. "I'm sor—"

"That's fine," Trevor said, raising a hand. He smiled through clear disappointment in his eyes, fatigue lines bracketing the corners of his mouth. "Those chairs by the lobby fireplace look comfortable enough to sleep on."

Marc worried his lip. Why did this feel so wrong? Leaving Trevor here alone, right before Christmas, to sleep in a chair? And why wasn't he just saying, *Thanks for a great night* and going on about his life, like he should be? Leaving a hookup shouldn't be that difficult. It should be simple. Except it wasn't.

They'd done more than spend a few hours finding release in each other. They'd talked for half the night, and he'd discovered he genuinely liked the man currently standing in front of him on a sunny but frigid Colorado morning. Trevor had somehow managed to touch

Marc in a way no one had in all his life. But . . . *hell*. How to tell a man he'd only meant to pass a night with that he didn't want to part ways so soon?

He ran his hands through his hair as Trevor watched him with an intensity that sent a shiver through this body.

They broke the nervous silence at the same time.

"Well—"

"Look, I—"

They laughed. He knew his sounded a touch shaky, but Trevor's sounded melancholy. Did he want what Marc did, too? Trevor looked toward the hotel doors, where a steady stream of taxis was shuttling people back to their cars or homes.

Marc squared his shoulders and opened his mouth to speak, but the words died on his lips when Trevor turned his attention back to him, expression unreadable, and held out his hand.

"I enjoyed meeting you, Marc. Thank you for a wonderful evening."

So, he didn't want what Marc did, then. He was eager to say good-bye and get on with his life. Because it was just a random one-night encounter, nothing more.

Marc stared at the extended hand for a second, reining in his useless fantasies, and met Trevor's eyes, searching for but not finding that spark that promised something more. He forced a smile that felt bittersweet but tasted only sour, and nodded, accepting Trevor's gesture.

"One I won't forget anytime soon," he said. He held on a moment longer and then let his hand slip slowly from Trevor's, fingertips caressing his palm as they broke contact, leaving tingling skin in the wake of a last touch. "Take care of yourself, Trevor. Merry Christmas."

Trevor pursed his lips slightly, suddenly looking wary, as if Marc had somehow just said the wrong thing. But all Trevor said was, "And to you."

The moment stretched on, standing almost frozen in time, until someone stepped into the edge of their private bubble and broke the spell.

"Your cab is here, sir," the concierge said.

Marc turned to the man. "Thank you," he said, then looked back at Trevor, smiled again, and with a sharp nod began walking toward the waiting cab. Every step felt heavier than the last, and he had to fight with himself not to turn around, walk back, say what he'd meant to say. But no, Trevor had made it clear. There was no more. He knew that too, but . . .

But there *was*.

Marc spun around with every intention of giving in to the urge and calling Trevor back, saying it was crazy but what the hell, let's see if this can go somewhere. But the spot where Trevor had been on the other side of the glass doors was now empty.

"Where to, sir?"

Marc turned back to the waiting cab driver, who was patiently holding the rear passenger-side door open.

"My car's on the turnpike," Marc said, climbing into the vehicle. He took one more glance back at the hotel, buckled his seat belt, and sighed. The empty wasteland that had become his life stretched farther than ever before, now beyond the horizon and into endless abyss.

Trevor headed for the lounge, fighting the urge to turn around and ask Marc to . . . What? Tell him he'll take that ride after all? But to where? He couldn't get up the mountain today, and there was no point in going to the airport. Ask Marc to stay at the hotel with him when the man had a home he could get to? And what about tomorrow? He'd been too caught up in the disappointment of missing Christmas with his family that he'd never actually asked what Marc's plans were, other than gathering he was spending it in town. From the sound of things, Marc didn't have family to spend it with, but surely he had friends to share the day.

But if he didn't . . . Wouldn't it be better to spend the day with someone whose company he'd thoroughly been enjoying than alone in a hotel full of strangers?

Inside the lounge, his gaze was immediately drawn to the table where he'd first sat with Marc, where a spell had been cast that had made him wish for a different life. For more time.

A heavy weight settled in his chest as he turned around and made his way toward the plush leather chairs that horseshoed in front of a large rock fireplace in the main lobby. He dropped into a chair, his body feeling twice as burdensome as usual, exhausted, as though he'd just run a marathon. He watched the flames jump and dance. Peripherally he was aware of movement around him, of people coming and going, of time inching eternally forward, but he sat still, wishing for things that could never be.

Just as well Marc had gone on his way. Trevor knew already he'd only want more of the man, even though he wouldn't fully be able to have him. He was already living on borrowed time, had been for a while. His damaged kidneys kept losing more and more function, and it wouldn't be long now before they failed completely, dialysis or not, without a transplant. Soon he'd no longer even be eligible for one.

That would be the height of selfishness, wouldn't it? No, he couldn't do that to anyone, least of all not a man like Marc.

He took a deep breath and dragged his sketchbook out of his bag. Settling the book on his lap, he flipped to the page where he'd drawn Marc in the silent hours of night. It was still a chaos of rough outlines simply giving the impression of form, but to Trevor, it was unmistakably Marc. His fingers twitched to trace the lines and curves of graphite, as if that were some sort of lifeline connecting him with a man he could only dream about from this point on.

With a sigh, he closed the book, placed both hands flat on the cover, and closed his eyes. He had to stop this. There were more important things to think about, like how to broach the topic with his mom that his kidneys were on the verge of a nosedive. Serious complications loomed large and fatal on the horizon, and he was considering stopping dialysis instead of putting them all through needless pain. That was not going to be an easy or pleasant conversation, but it was one that couldn't be avoided.

"Mind if I join you?"

The resonant voice had a smile in it, and Trevor would have recognized it anywhere. He snapped his eyes open, and there before him stood Mr. Marc Handsome. In the flesh.

A distant voice in Trevor's mind expressed gratitude that he had closed his sketchbook. He stood up, dropping the pad to the seat of the chair without thought.

"What are you doing here?" His voice cracked, but he didn't care. A sense of joy and hope he couldn't possibly suppress rose in his chest, and for a moment, he didn't even want to try.

Marc shoved his hands in his pockets and looked down, his expression and movements uncertain, revealing chinks in his confidence. When he once again met Trevor's gaze, the hope Trevor was feeling was reflected back at him in shades of warm green.

"I, uh . . . I was thinking . . ." Marc pulled his hands free and rolled his shoulders back, his voice more assured as he continued. "I was thinking it's not right for you to spend your Christmas alone in a hotel lobby, sleeping in a damn chair, while I spend mine alone in the foothills, when we could spend it together. No one should be alone on Christmas, right?"

"I . . ."

. . . *can't. Shouldn't. But yes, I want to.*

"My house is big," he added. "You'd have your choice of guest rooms, if you wish. Though"—a playful light danced in Marc's eyes—"I have a very large master bedroom."

He waited for a response, that playful light returning to the previous hopeful expression, but at Trevor's hesitation, that began to fade. Trevor hated knowing that he was the cause of it, but he couldn't go to Marc's home. It wasn't that he didn't want to spend the holiday there, to simply be with him, it was that the more time he spent with him, the harder it would be to say good-bye. And good-bye was the only place this could go.

"I can't . . ." he started, letting his voice trail off at the crestfallen look on Marc's face. Trevor's heart twisted at the image, giving the offer a second thought just to make that look go away. The man was right, after all. No one should spend Christmas alone, and he had nowhere to go. As long as they were on the same page, it would be okay. Right? Just a couple of guys making the most of the situation. Then when the airport reopened, he'd head home as planned, and this would have been a memorable interlude.

You're fooling yourself, a voice whispered in the depths of his psyche, which he promptly ignored. He swallowed.

"I'm not looking for anything here," he said, his voice firm as he locked eyes with Marc. "As long as we're clear."

Conflicting emotions bounced through Marc's eyes, changing too quickly to get a read on any particular one, but his voice was eager when he said, "We're clear. I definitely don't have time for anything more right now, either." Marc smiled, a grin so beautiful and sincere that it washed away every reason Trevor should have said no.

"Okay. Take me home, then."

CHAPTER TEN

"We'll need to stop at the grocery store on the way," Marc said as he steered his late-model Audi Q7 onto Interlocken Boulevard, heading back toward the Boulder Turnpike. "I don't eat at home often enough to actually stock the kitchen. Is there anywhere you need to stop on the way? Anything you need?"

Trevor shook his head. The only thing he really needed Marc couldn't give him. "Do you not cook?"

A snort of a laugh escaped Marc. "Not much point."

"Of course there is. Everyone has to eat."

"And that's why we have a city full of restaurants and great takeout," Marc said. He was still smiling, but it looked a little forced, a little lonely.

Trevor studied Marc's profile for a moment. Sunglasses sat on the bridge of a perfectly straight nose, a dusting of dark stubble followed the angle of a strong jaw, and a tongue poked out to slide along a plump lower lip that Trevor knew firsthand felt like satin. He was intelligent, driven, successful . . . gorgeous. Why was a man like this alone?

Sure, Trevor was alone when it came to romantic relationships, too, but with damn good reason. If a transplant didn't come through for him soon, he could very possibly be dead in a year. Even if he did get a new one, there was no guarantee his body would even accept it. But he had family and good friends to fulfill his life. What did Marc have other than work?

An ache trickled into his chest when he remembered what Marc had told him in the dark last night, about being a ghost in his own home. Trevor couldn't imagine what that must have been like, having always had the unwavering and unconditional love, support, and encouragement of his own family.

"I'm going to cook for you then," Trevor decided aloud. This couldn't go anywhere, but that didn't mean he couldn't help someone feel a little less alone. Even if just for a day. "I mean, it's the least I can do, since you're being kind enough to invite a wayward stranger into your home for Christmas."

Marc glanced over at him, his smile soft. Trevor couldn't see his eyes behind the mirrored shades, but his voice was pure honey when he said, "Not really a stranger anymore."

Trevor smiled back. Nothing about Marc felt like a stranger to him, even though it had been less than twenty-four hours since they'd met. How could that be? Fate, his mom would say. Her belief in love at first sight and "just knowing" when you've met the one you're supposed to be with was unshakable. But that was his mom. Not him. He already knew miracles didn't happen, and fate could be a fickle bitch.

Marc reached over, as if he was going to take Trevor's hand in his, but he paused midway, moving to grip the steering wheel instead. He returned his focus to the road ahead of them, and his Adam's apple bobbed as he swallowed.

I'd have held your hand.

Trevor gave himself a mental knock on the head to stay in check. He shifted his gaze out the window, where a thick blanket of pristine white powder covered the passing land. The fresh snow glistening under the bright winter sun—still, pure, peaceful—that never failed to awe him with its quiet beauty. He burned the image, the tone of its mood, to memory so he could paint it later. The idea took shape in his mind's eye as they drove—a big canvas, maybe six feet by four, the bottom third a stark snow-covered landscape littered with diamonds, and a vast blue sky that reached for eternity filling out the rest of the canvas.

Before he knew it, they were pulling into Boulder's local organic grocer—open but minimally staffed due to the blizzard—where Trevor gathered ingredients to make a few renal-diet-friendly meals. The added bonus of cooking for Marc was that he could control the menu and wouldn't have to explain why there were so many foods he couldn't eat. He didn't want to get into his condition, didn't want to talk about it . . . really didn't want to even think about it. Right now he just wanted to focus on enjoying the company of an attractive, kind man.

"Do you have any food allergies? Or anything in particular you don't like?" Trevor asked as he picked out a package of skinless chicken thighs. He tossed the package into their cart and tried to ignore how domestic grocery shopping with Marc felt.

This was a mistake. He should have stayed at the hotel.

And slept in a chair? the devil on his shoulder chided.

"I'm a garbage can," Marc said, bestowing a smile on him that could compete with the sun. "I'll eat anything."

Damn it. Why did those smiles make Trevor ignore the things he couldn't afford to forget? At least he'd already verbally set the boundaries and Marc had agreed—neither of them was looking for more.

"I'm not sure if I should be impressed or appalled," Trevor teased, hoping a little humor would get him out of his own head.

"Impressed." Marc's eyes danced with infectious mirth. "Definitely."

Trevor shook his head and grinned. "Appalling," he said, making sure his tone was playful.

Marc's gaze dropped to Trevor's mouth, and even as he resisted the urge to lick his lips, he wasn't able to turn away. Marc's eyes flicked up, connected with Trevor's, and for that brief moment the only sound he could hear was the buzzing of electricity sparking between them.

Trevor cleared his throat. "Just a . . . a few more things and . . ." He nodded, as though that would break down the roadblock his tongue suddenly seemed unable to navigate. He turned away before Marc could say anything and quickly gathered the rest of the food.

Twenty minutes later, Marc pulled over at the foot of a long, snow-covered drive that led to a sprawling rancher. Snowplows had been along the main road at some point, but the entrance to the drive was blocked by a good four feet of pile up. Marc sighed and killed the engine, turning to him with an apologetic expression. "I'm sorry. It looks like we're hiking it from here."

"No problem," Trevor said, his legs needing the stretch anyway. "The fresh air will do us good."

"I've got an ATV with a plow on it to clear the drive." Marc opened his door, and cold air burst its way inside. "I'll get changed after we get everything inside and take care of that. Shovel open this fancy new gate, too, so I can get the car off the road."

"If you've got two shovels, I'll help."

Marc smiled. "Thanks." He grabbed their two bags of groceries, while Trevor threw his duffel bag over his shoulder, and together they trudged their way through the powdery snow and up the drive.

His breath puffed out ahead of him, as if leading the way, and snow crept between his pant legs and socks to chill his ankles. Even though he exercised regularly, he was winded by the time they reached the house, and his legs were ready to give out. While constant fatigue had become a normal state of being for him since starting dialysis, he wasn't usually this wiped out after his treatments anymore. But the last twenty-four hours had been a little out of his regular routine, what with the late night and amazing sex—not just once, but twice. He shook his head. He still couldn't believe how Marc had gotten his libido so charged up. Now though, the fatigue had seeped deep and made his bones feel heavy. If he could sneak in a nap, he'd be okay the rest of the day.

Side by side they stomped up two short steps to a sprawling front porch, and he set his bag down by the door, then shook the snow from his pants. Marc did the same before gathering the bags and opening the front door. Anxiety snaked into Trevor's chest as he followed Marc into a large foyer that revealed an open floor plan and a west wall banked in floor-to-ceiling windows. The Front Range mountains stood tall and majestic in the frame of the windows, and Trevor's breath caught, awe replacing the sudden bout of apprehension. This view alone was well worth the unplanned hike.

He whistled. "Wow."

Marc glanced over his shoulder and smiled. "That's the number one reason why I bought this place. That and the East Boulder trails are just outside."

"Impressive," Trevor said, dropping his bag to the floor. He kicked off his shoes, hung his jacket on a hook by the door, and followed

Marc into a massive chef's kitchen. "How can you have a kitchen like this and not cook?" He shook his head.

Marc looked around the kitchen, almost as if he were seeing it for the first time. "I'd intended to use it often, but . . ." He shrugged and then began emptying the contents of the grocery bags.

It seemed he wasn't going to continue, and Trevor had the distinct impression he shouldn't press. Instead, he helped unpack the groceries, handing items to Marc who put them in their assigned places, in companionable silence. He tried again not to think about how domestic it all felt. He definitely did not think about how right it felt. A life like this wasn't, and would never be, his.

"Come on," Marc said when they were done. "Let me give you the grand tour, then we'll change and head back out."

"Lead the way, squire," Trevor teased, grateful for the distraction from his wandering mind.

The house was gorgeous. His own home up in Nederland didn't have the expansive views, being surrounded by trees as it was, but he'd always thought he'd had a king's ransom in natural light with skylights in nearly every room. The light that filtered into this house put his to shame, though. Not only were there multiple skylights in almost every room but each window ran floor to ceiling, and the ceilings? Vaulted with natural wood and exposed beams. Everything about this home was bright, open, and airy. It was beautifully appointed with a welcoming, homey mood to it, but the feeling that something was missing nudged at him. That this was a house on the verge of being a home. After a few minutes he realized the walls were devoid of photos—not a single family portrait, no candid snapshots of friends celebrating or vacation memories. Not to mention . . .

"You don't have a Christmas tree," he blurted, and immediately heat charged into his cheeks.

Marc looked down, shoving his hands into his pocket. Trevor'd embarrassed the man. "Yeah. Not really here much to enjoy it, or, you know . . . it's just me."

"I'm sorry. I didn't mean—"

"No, it's okay." Marc met his eyes and smiled, but his expression read unsure. "Maybe we can do something to festive the place up together?"

"I—" Trevor frowned. "What?" Marc wanted them to decorate his house together? That was . . . *I am* not *going to say domestic again.*

"Or . . ." Marc turned away, but not before Trevor caught the lush green of his eyes dim. "My apologies. That was silly."

"No, *I'm* sorry," Trevor said quickly. The last thing he wanted was for Marc to think him an ungrateful asshole. He reached out, placing his hand on Marc's biceps and giving the firm muscle beneath his palm a brief squeeze. Not getting involved didn't mean they couldn't do things together, right? It didn't have to be any different than helping to decorate the little art gallery in Nederland. "I didn't mean to put you on the spot about not having decorated or for seeming not to want to. It was just . . . I don't know. But . . . it's a good idea."

Marc glanced back at him, studying him for a second before he placed his hand over Trevor's.

"More to see," Marc said quietly, his voice thick, and tipped his head toward a short set of stairs. He dropped his hand, turning to finish the tour, and Trevor fell in step behind him, hoping he wouldn't stick his foot in his mouth again.

The ranch-style house had been built on the side of a hill, so there wasn't a basement, but there was a lower level on one side. Marc stopped at the bottom of the stairwell, and Trevor walked past him into another large open space. Sitting directly below the main living area on the upper level, a bank of windows surrounded French doors facing the same view of the Front Range. Blue sky made brighter by the crisp snow stretched miles high.

The opposite wall was off-white and completely bare. The far side of the space was lined with shelves and drawers. At the other end of the room was a sitting area with a comfortable-looking chaise, two chairs, and a wooden table in the middle. But what caught and demanded his attention was what stood in the middle of the room, facing the view: an easel with a large blank canvas on it.

Trevor turned to Marc, opening his mouth to ask why it sat there blank, why the room seemed so . . . abandoned, and why that perfectly lit gallery wall was empty, but the words died before he'd finished taking a full breath to speak them. Marc wasn't looking at him, still hadn't even entered the room. In fact, he'd retreated back up to the lower step. His gaze was fixed on the view beyond the window, as if he were deliberately not looking into the room, and the rigid stance of his body said he wanted out of there as fast as possible.

It didn't make sense to Trevor. To have this incredible space, to have it set up specifically as an *art* space, but to pretend it wasn't there?

Then he remembered what Marc had said in the middle of the night: that he'd wanted to be an artist, but disapproval from his mother had made him bury his true dreams. Marc had said he had no time to get back into art now, but this room . . . Trevor's heart squeezed tight in his chest. This room was a silent cry.

Marc shot a quick glance at Trevor. "Ready for the grand finale?" he asked, his voice tight.

"Sure." But Marc was halfway up the steps before Trevor finished the single word. If only he could help make this man's life better . . . If only he had enough time to make a difference . . . They had today and tomorrow, though. That would have to be enough.

He followed Marc around a corner and into what had to be the biggest master bedroom—no, master *suite*—he'd ever seen.

"If I didn't know any better, I'd swear you planned this tour to end here," Trevor said, stopping behind Marc in the large room. Just as all the other rooms in this house, two full walls were windows. Another set of French doors opened out to a patio that ran the length of the eastern side of the house, and sunlight shone down through three skylights.

"Are you suggesting I had ulterior motives?" Marc's voice was pitched low, husky, and he turned and snaked a finger through Trevor's belt loop, tugging him closer. An impish light sparked in his eyes.

Trevor grinned. "Depends what those motives are."

"I have a feeling you might like them." Marc dipped his head and nipped at Trevor's lips. The touch sent a charge of shivers racing through his body.

"There can't be any more to this," Trevor reminded him, steadfastly ignoring the part of him that *did* want more.

Marc tilted his head slightly, and Trevor could see the wheels turning in his brain. He braced himself for questions he would not answer.

"We're on the same page," Marc finally said, but he didn't let go of Trevor's belt loop.

"Good." And it *was* good, so why was his relief tinged with disappointment?

Marc pulled Trevor closer until their bodies bumped against each other. "Doesn't mean we can't take advantage of the moment," he said. His solid body pressed against the length of Trevor's, and this time Trevor initiated the next move.

The kiss was slow, sensual, and he opened his mouth to welcome Marc's tongue inside. Trevor angled his head to deepen the kiss, and Marc responded with an intensity that would have knocked Trevor's shoes off had he still been wearing them. He was being devoured, and he loved every second of it, wanted more, wanted it always. And right now, he didn't care what that meant. He just wanted to feel.

But Marc broke the kiss, calming the fire that was building between them, and stepped back. A chill stole over Trevor from the absence of all that hard heat against him, and he stumbled a step forward. His chest rising and falling rapidly as air puffed from his lungs in small gusts, and his mind raced to catch up with what had just happened.

A wicked grin pulled at Marc's mouth. "First we shovel, then we play," he said, his voice gruff. He walked over to a chest of drawers and pulled out a T-shirt and pair of sweatpants, tipping a chin at Trevor before tossing the clothing his way.

Trevor fumbled but somehow managed to catch the clothes to his chest. "Evil . . . No wonder lawyers have such a bad rap."

After clearing the drive with the ATV, they shoveled the snow bank at the end so Marc could get his car off the road. Trevor rode the ATV back to the house while Marc drove the car. As he pulled into the garage and killed the engine, something Kate had said the day before danced into his mind.

"Have you ever built a snowman?" Marc asked as he exited the car.

Trevor looked at him over the roof of the car and smiled. "Every year."

"Still?" He retrieved the snow shovels from the back of the ATV.

"Still." Trevor took one of the shovels and followed him, returning them to their designated place in the garage. "Between my brothers and sisters, and now nieces and nephews, we divide into two teams and then try to outdo each other with the best snowman. Mom and Dad do the judging, but somehow it always ends up being a tie." He winked.

An odd ache drifted into Marc's chest. Was it jealousy? Grief for the loss of something he'd never had?

"Sounds like a lot of fun," he said, making an effort to keep his voice even.

He must not have succeeded, however, because Trevor studied him for a second before he spoke. "Have you never built a snowman?"

Marc shook his head. "I grew up in Arizona, near Phoenix. We don't get a lot of snow there."

"Too bad the snow is too dry here to stick. Unless we add water and make an iceman . . .?" Trevor raised an eyebrow.

"No, no." Marc laughed. "I don't need to make one that bad."

Trevor didn't say anything, just stood there looking at him as though he was trying to puzzle him out. The blue of his eyes was as crisp and endless as the winter skies outside, yet only warmth drifted from them, folding around Marc's body, weaving into his bones, filling all the empty corners. It was a chance encounter that would only survive a brief moment in time, but what this man was doing to him . . .

"Actually," Marc said, stepping close enough to breathe in Trevor's arousing scent—fresh and invigorating, as if he'd somehow bottled the sun and the mountains, and a raw undernote that had warmth spreading into Marc's groin. "I have a better idea that doesn't involve ice and snow and freezing our butts off."

They'd sweat enough from clearing the driveway to warrant getting naked together in the shower for a second time that day, as far as he was concerned. He reached for Trevor's hand, and hesitation flickered in his eyes.

Trevor continued to study him, and for a second, Marc thought he wouldn't accept his offer, but then he slipped his hand into Marc's. The skin was cool, even though he'd worn thick gloves while shoveling.

"You're going to wear me out," Trevor warned, but there was a note of anticipation in his voice.

"Only in the best way." Marc exhaled a breath he couldn't remember holding and led Trevor inside, not stopping until they reached the large shower in his master bath. He leaned in, kissing and nibbling on full lips he was already becoming addicted to, and when he opened his mouth, Trevor didn't hesitate to accept the invitation. The rush of the other man's taste flooded him with desire and dreams. Things he'd put aside, things he didn't have time for.

Trevor pulled back, snaked his hands under Marc's T-shirt, and slid it up his torso, nudging his arms up to remove the piece of clothing, but those now hot, branding hands remained on his skin.

"I can't believe how easily you get me hard," Trevor said in a husky voice that sent a shiver of longing up and down Marc's spine. "This never happens."

"The feeling is mutual," he whispered, making quick work of helping Trevor out of his clothes while Trevor pushed Marc's sweatpants to the floor. Then Trevor's mouth was back on his. Kissing, nipping with a touch of teeth, tongue sliding inside—hot and passionate and demanding—and without breaking apart, Marc led Trevor into the shower.

Leaning down to turn on the water, he kissed Trevor's chin, the column of his neck, his collarbone, over a solid pectoral. They both jumped at the cold blast of water from the showerhead above them, and laughing, Marc pulled Trevor out of the spray until it warmed up.

He slid his hands over Trevor's shoulders and along his toned arms, but two lumps under the skin of his left biceps—where the gauze had been wrapped previously—drew Marc's attention. Raised flesh surrounded what looked like puncture marks. "What happened here?"

Trevor tensed, pulling his arm back, but Marc held on, letting his hands slide the rest of the way down Trevor's arms in a caress he hoped would be understood. Whatever it was, it didn't lessen how badly he wanted this man.

"I'm sorry; I didn't mean to pry. Just curious." Marc stepped closer, threading their fingers together, and gently kissed Trevor.

"No, it's okay. It's just . . ." Trevor looked down and shrugged before meeting his eyes again, expression closed. "Nothing to worry about."

Marc nodded. It could be his own perceptions coloring things, but if he wasn't mistaken he'd seen a flash of fear in those bright-blue eyes. Whatever had caused those marks, Trevor would tell him if he wanted to. Marc wouldn't push, but a small part of him wanted Trevor to trust him enough *to* want to talk about it.

"Water's good," Trevor said, his voice a touch shaky. He stepped past Marc to stand under the stream, reaching for the soap.

Marc slipped his arms around Trevor's waist and pulled their bodies flush, chest to back, and kissed the nape of Trevor's neck. He moaned and dropped his head back onto Marc's shoulder. "That feels good."

"Yeah?"

"You know it."

Marc rolled his hips until his penis settled nicely between Trevor's buttocks. Trevor reached back, one hand covering a butt cheek, and tugged Marc closer while the other guided Marc's hand down Trevor's belly to his groin. That was guidance Marc would gladly take. He cupped Trevor's balls with his right and began caressing the length of his cock with his left. Trevor wiggled, changing the angle in order to squeeze his legs together and trap Marc's now fully hard and aching cock between them in a perfect, slick grip.

"God. Seriously." Marc groaned, the sweet pressure and hot, wet friction on his cock making it hard to think. "How have we not met before?" *How have we not been taking showers like this for years now?*

Trevor answered by angling his head back to capture Marc's mouth in a frantic kiss, and all Marc could do was hang on tight. His legs shook, his body trembled, his blood sang, and together they rocked in unison. Synchronized motion and panting increasing until their bodies and combined voices reached crescendo, rivaling the patter of hot water sluicing over their even hotter skin.

Marc carved a trail of kisses over Trevor's shoulder, up the side of his neck, and then tugged the shell of his ear into his mouth. "So far, best Christmas ever."

Trevor chuckled low and deep in his chest, and it was one of the most erotic sounds Marc had ever heard. He tightened his arms around Trevor, pulling him as close as possible, and rested his chin on Trevor's shoulder. They stood like that for a moment, bodies pressed together, and nothing had ever felt more right to Marc.

But he wasn't ready for that kind of "right" in his life.

"C'mon." Marc released Trevor and, stepping back, gave his ass a playful smack. "I think we're clean enough for dinner."

But after they'd dried off and dressed, Trevor sat down on the edge of the bed, looking exhausted. Marc had been so pumped at the idea of spending more time with Trevor that he hadn't realized how little they'd slept the night before, nor had he noticed the dark circles beneath those bright eyes that had now gone dull and distant.

"Are you feeling okay?" he asked.

Trevor jerked back from wherever he'd gone, the light returning, but the smile on his face didn't quite match his eyes.

"Yes," he said a bit too quickly and then shook his head. He released a breath on a sigh that seemed like it had been held in for too long. "To be honest, I'm feeling a little tired."

"Why don't you take a nap, and I'll get dinner ready for us?" Marc stepped forward and rested a hand on Trevor's shoulder.

Trevor eyed him dubiously. "I thought you didn't cook?"

"Just because I *don't* cook doesn't mean I *can't*." Marc winked. He reached up to caress Trevor's cheek without even thinking about it. He pulled his hand back. "Besides, you're on Christmas dinner duty tomorrow."

"Okay." Trevor smiled. "Thank you. I was going to make cranberry chicken with white rice and green beans, but you can do something else if you want."

"No, that sounds perfect."

With a nod and a smile, Marc turned to gather their wet towels and throw them in the hamper in the bathroom. When he walked back into the bedroom, Trevor had already crawled under the covers and curled up. He must have been more than a little tired to have passed out that quickly. Marc went over and pulled the blankets up a little more, feeling the need to tuck them under Trevor's chin, and then stood back. He looked natural, right, there in Marc's bed. In

Marc's house. As if he belonged there. Everything about Trevor felt right, really.

Marc brushed a stray lock of hair back from Trevor's forehead and then left him to his slumber. He had to shake a little rust out of his cooking skills and see if he could pull off the meal Trevor had intended, lest he send the man running for the hills.

He would *not* analyze why that mattered later.

CHAPTER ELEVEN

*I*nsistent morning sunlight teased Trevor's eyes open, and disorientation quickly followed. Instead of the thick pine forest that usually greeted him through his bedroom window, his vision was filled with a majestic view of white-blanketed farmland and endless blue skies. He sat up with a start and looked around the large room, the floor-to-ceiling windows beyond the foot of the oversized bed he was in, and he remembered. Against his better judgment, he had gone home with a man he'd met while stranded during a blizzard.

And he'd slept through the dinner that man had been making for him. *Shit.*

He threw his legs over the side of the bed and glanced back over his shoulder. The bed sheets on the other side were in disarray. Not only had he slept through dinner and the entire night, but Marc had apparently slept right beside him, and he hadn't even stirred.

With a sigh, he put his ear to his left biceps, listening to the thrill of blood as it flowed through the dialysis access point of the fistula in his arm. Everything sounded okay, which was good considering he'd managed to completely forget checking yesterday. The very last thing he needed right now was for a clot to form.

Getting up to retrieve his bag—and the ten different medications, binders, and vitamins within—he noticed a plate of strawberries and cheese, garnished with a sprig of fresh mint on the night table. His stomach grumbled. Beside the morning snack was a glass of water, as well as a glass of orange juice.

Damn it. Why did Marc have to be so thoughtful?

Sitting back down, he passed on the OJ—the potassium he was always trying to keep balanced would be thrown off by it—opting for the water instead, and swallowed his pills. Then he eyed the cheese. As much as he should avoid it as well, he loved cheese too much. Besides, his renal dietitian said "should" avoid it, not "must always." There were only a couple of small cubes. A little deviation wouldn't kill him. Not yet, anyway. And should he end up deciding to go off dialysis, he was going to eat everything and anything he hadn't been able to for the last seven years.

When he finished the cheese and fruit plate, he pulled on a pair of jeans and a Henley, topping it with a light sweater. He gathered up the dishes and made his way to the kitchen, an annoying sense of anticipation creeping in with each step. He should not have come here. He'd been too attracted to Marc from the start, had enjoyed the man's company too much, and that shower yesterday afternoon . . . A part of him knew he was dangerously close to ignoring his situation and enjoying what Marc had to offer. He couldn't let that happen. What he should be doing is grabbing his bag and going to a hotel until he could get a flight out, or home if the road up the canyon was accessible now.

He rounded the corner to see Marc sitting at the dining room table in front of a laptop, file folders and papers spread out around him. He looked up, and the smile Trevor found himself graced with sent a wave of warmth rushing through his veins and cascading over his skin. Which was quickly followed by the chill ache of loss and impossible wishes. How could there be a god, if one were so cruel as to put a man like Marc into his life just as it was coming to an end?

"There you are," Marc said, rising from the table and crossing the room. "I was giving you another half hour before I came in to make sure you were still alive."

I'm alive for now, anyway. "I am so sorry to have passed out on you like that."

Marc waved him off. "Don't worry about it. You obviously needed it."

"Yeah," Trevor said, turning to put the plate and juice glass on the counter. Strong arms wrapped around his torso. He knew he shouldn't do this, but he couldn't seem to step out of Marc's embrace, either. Just a hug. Simple human touch. That's all. Didn't have to be any more to it than that. Reluctantly, he let Marc turn him until they faced each other.

"Marc . . ." He'd meant to remind him that this wasn't going anywhere, meant to step back and put safe space between them, but only a soft sigh drifted past his lips and then Marc's mouth was pressing against them. He breathed the man in, wanting to stop but wishing he could give everything, and lost himself in the languid kiss.

"Damn, you taste good," Marc whispered as they parted, his voice gravely.

"Strawberries. In winter, even," Trevor said, trying not to show how off-balance this whole thing had him. "Thank you for the morning appetizer, by the way."

"My pleasure," Marc said, squeezing Trevor more tightly. He didn't seem to want to let go, and Trevor found he wasn't able to as his emotions took the reins from his brain. He let his hands roam over Marc's back, skin hot through the fabric of his heavy shirt and down to the curve of his firm butt. Trevor didn't know who had started it, but they began a slow sway where they stood—not quite a dance but so, so nice.

"How about I make us break—"

"How about *I* make us breakfast," Trevor interrupted and smiled sheepishly. "Since I went and slept through dinner last night. And then we'll entertain ourselves by doing something about the serious lack of holiday cheer in this house." Anything that would keep them busy and out of bedrooms or showers.

Marc smiled and kissed him again. "Sounds good to me."

He sat on the other side of the island, elbows on the counter, hands clasped under his chin while Trevor set about gathering the ingredients for a vegetable omelet. He desperately needed the distraction from things he couldn't have but wanted anyway.

He tipped his head toward the abandoned computer on the table as he pulled a knife from the rack on the counter and started slicing mushrooms. "Please don't tell me you're working on a holiday?"

Marc raised his hands in surrender. "Guilty, but no more now that you're up." A blush crept into his cheeks. "And truth be told, I . . . uh . . . I tried to google you while you were sleeping."

"No wonder I feel so dirty," Trevor said, making sure his tone sounded light and teasing as an unwelcome wave of delight washed through him.

"Ugh." Marc ducked his head. "I'm sorry. That sounded creepy."

"No! Not at all." Trevor laughed, pushing the chopped mushrooms aside and grabbing a green pepper. "Well, a little. But I'm actually flattered."

Marc shifted on his seat and lifted his eyes. When their gazes connected Trevor could have sworn sparks shot out between them. "I wanted to see your artwork."

"And did you find me?"

"There's only one artist in the Boulder Art Gallery named Trevor. Trevor Morrison. That would be you, yes?"

Trevor nodded.

"I did, then," he said with a smile. "And your work is amazing."

Now Trevor was the one to blush. He turned to toss the mushrooms and peppers into a pan and started on the broccoli. "Thank you."

"I love how you use a palette knife instead of brushes, and your choice of vibrant colors is captivating. Oh, and the mood you evoke with *The Lonely Hour* . . ."

Trevor looked over his shoulder when Marc trailed off. He was staring out the window, his gaze distant again, lost in whatever thoughts the painting had inspired in him. Trevor hoped they were good thoughts.

"The empty bench in that painting is a quiet place to sit and contemplate, search for answers, to welcome something new into life," Trevor said, remembering how young he'd been when he'd painted that one, how he'd felt like the whole world awaited him. Less than a year later his kidneys began to fail. "I sat there on that very bench myself. It's in front of a corner park in Paris."

Marc met his gaze, smiled, but Trevor could see the wheels spinning behind those heart-melting eyes. Suddenly feeling on the spot, Trevor turned back to his breakfast task, breaking two eggs into the frying pan and mixing them in with the veggies. He startled when arms wrapped around his waist from behind, but then settled against the warm body at his back without making the conscious decision to do so. Moist breath tickled the nape of his neck before soft lips pressed a kiss to his skin.

"You're a beautiful man." Marc's voice was a rasp, barely audible, and screaming with such raw yearning that Trevor had to grip the edge of the counter to keep himself upright. "I'm glad I met you, and I am honored you came to spend this day with me. I know we agreed this would just be what it is, but say there can be more than this."

Trevor closed his eyes, squeezed them tight, and swallowed hard against a lump that had formed in his throat. Part of him so badly wanted to say yes—oh God, did he—but there was no way he could. "I can't . . ." His voice cracked. "There can't be more. I'm sorry."

Marc was still for a long moment, his arms wrapped loosely around Trevor's waist, and then he nodded. "I understand." Those soft lips pressed lightly against the side of Trevor's neck again, and then Marc let go and stepped back. Trevor fought the shiver that trembled under the surface of his skin from the loss. He was doing the right thing and he knew it, so why did it feel so wrong?

CHAPTER TWELVE

$\mathcal{M}$arc plodded through the deep, powdery snow, not really paying attention to his surroundings. Trevor walked beside him. Their conversion over breakfast still played in his mind. He hadn't intended to ask for more, hadn't known he even wanted that, but he couldn't regret it now. Yes, he'd told Trevor he was on the same page, that this was just a one-night thing, albeit extended to a couple of days now, with good reason. Otherwise, Trevor would have been sitting alone in a hotel lobby or the crowded floors of the airport.

He hadn't been looking for anything nor had he wanted anything, but in the course of two days, the page had turned when he hadn't been looking. He suddenly knew what Kate meant when she'd claimed there was more to life than work.

And Marc knew the page had turned for Trevor, too. He had said he *couldn't* let this be more, not that he didn't *want* it to be. The signs were all there in his body language, in the light in his eyes, the inflections in his voice. Any trial attorney worth his salt could see it. So what held Trevor back? What made him say there couldn't be more? Wasn't Trevor the one who said you had to make the time for the important things?

"There! That's the one."

The shout snapped Marc from his ponderings, and he looked over to see Trevor pointing at a small ponderosa pine. The tiny tree was a little on the Charlie Brown side, maybe three feet tall with thinned-out branches, but Trevor's infectious exuberance made it the best-looking tree Marc had ever seen. Not a chance was he going to risk dimming that light by not agreeing.

"That one it is, then," Marc said, laughing as Trevor trudged through the snow ahead of him.

Marc caught up with him and stopped at Trevor's side, his breath puffing out in gossamer clouds. Trevor met his eyes, smile stretching from cheek to cheek, and dug his shovel through fluffy snow and into hard ground.

Marc frowned. "Tell me again why we aren't just cutting it down?"

"Catch and release," Trevor said, his voice serious.

"What?" Marc laughed. "It's not a fish!"

"No, but it is alive. Why kill it for a few days' enjoyment, when you can replant it and enjoy it for the rest of your life? In twenty years this bad boy will be a good thirty feet tall."

"I guess it makes sense," Marc said, driving his shovel into the ground on the other side.

"What's that?"

"That an artist would be a tree hugger," Marc teased, unable to keep the grin off of his face.

Trevor tossed a shovel full of snow at him, laughing. "Get to work, you."

Marc dusted himself off, and then they both began digging up the tree as if they were digging for gold.

With their tree freed from the frozen earth, they placed it on a larger burlap sack Trevor had found in Marc's garage, and dragged it back to the house. Marc smiled the whole way, and for the first time in years, a joy and wonder that he thought he'd lost forever bubbled up inside him. He looked over the tip of the tree at Trevor, who turned to face him with a wide smile, and the world brightened another notch. He didn't say anything and neither did Trevor. The moment didn't need words because it was right there in eyes as blue as the sky above.

Marc was still smiling when they carried the tree into the house and settled it into a planter near the fireplace in the great room, facing the Front Range. He stood back and put his hands on his hips. "There's just one problem."

Standing beside him, Trevor mirrored his pose. "What's that?"

He looked over at his houseguest. "I don't have anything to decorate it with."

Trevor bumped his shoulder against Marc's. "You have paint downstairs. And you have popcorn and string, don't you?"

"I do."

"Then that's what we'll start with." Trevor kissed his cheek and then gave him a playful shove toward the kitchen. "You put on some music and get the popcorn started. I'll get the turkey in the oven, and then we'll decorate the tree together."

This was something he could do for Marc. It wasn't much, and he might not even catch on to Trevor's motive, but it could be that little spark Marc needed to rediscover his passion for art, regardless.

After making sure the small turkey was on track for dinner in a few hours, he went to retrieve his sketchbook, and graphite and colored pencils. It'd be easy to make ornaments out of his supplies. Marc was dumping the popcorn into a bowl when he returned to the kitchen, and a small ball of tricolored string sat on the counter next to it. He looked up from his task and smiled.

"Want to do this downstairs?" Trevor asked, and Marc's smile slipped. "Your studio space is perfect. No need to risk getting paint on your nice furniture up here."

Marc didn't look convinced. In fact, he looked downright uncomfortable. "What are we doing exactly?"

"Decorating your tree."

"The tree is up here."

"Just trust me." Trevor grinned and motioned toward the stairs with a tilt of his head. "Grab the popcorn and let's go."

Marc sighed but didn't argue. Doing as bid—even though he clearly didn't like the idea—he followed Trevor down to the neglected art studio. Unease radiated off the man in thick waves, and a well of anger rose in Trevor's chest, startling him by how fast it came to the surface and how intensely. He'd never been one to have a quick temper, but maybe helplessness at his own situation had been brewing ignored and now he had a focus for it that didn't involve the *Should I stop dialysis and when?* questions. In that moment he turned all his impotent fury on Marc's mother. What kind of parent crushed her son's dreams, his soul, like that? Or rejected any part of him for any reason and made him feel so insignificant? How a person could do something like that wasn't even within his grasp of reasoning.

If Trevor's mom could have adopted Marc, she would have in a heartbeat. She would have loved him, encouraged him to follow his every dream, and been right beside him the whole way. An overwhelming urge to take Marc home to meet his mom engulfed him. He tried to tamp it down.

If only he had *time*.

But Marc wouldn't ever be meeting his mom. There would never be more than these couple of days with him. Worse than that, now that he'd met the man, spent time with him, he would always know what his fucking kidneys and his damn blood type had cost him.

Trevor pointed to the chairs and table at the end of the room. "Let's set up over there," he said, needing to get away from the dark path his thoughts were taking, and focus on reintroducing Marc to the joys of creating. Even if it was only to make Christmas decorations.

Marc remained quiet as Trevor spread out his art supplies before gathering a mix of watercolor and acrylic paint from the shelves. He hadn't noticed the day before that there was a small powder room discretely set behind the shelving unit, complete with paint-cleaning supplies, water containers, and various palettes. He shook his head, again marveling at how someone could make a point of building the perfect art studio, yet never set foot inside it.

Satisfied they had everything they needed, Trevor sat down across from Marc. "Ready?"

But Marc clearly wasn't. He sat there looking at Trevor, his expression so vulnerable, so lost, that a need to fill all his empty spaces with light and happiness and belonging tugged at Trevor's chest.

"What do you want to start with?" Trevor whispered. He needed Marc to choose, needed to coax his artist's soul out from the dungeon he'd locked it in.

Marc looked down at the table, a frown curving his mouth. He reached out and ran a shaky finger over the handle of a brush, then a graphite pencil, and on to the colored-pencil set, fingertips touching every color as if they held secret messages. He moved back to the paintbrushes and selected a filbert tip, holding it in his hand as though he'd just discovered a lost treasure. Which, as far as Trevor was concerned, he had.

Trevor smiled when their gazes reconnected. "Let's paint. Then we'll string popcorn."

Marc nodded, and together they began painting festive designs on the paper from Trevor's sketchbook in companionable silence. Marc's first attempt was . . . abstract. Splashes and splatters of greens, reds, blues, and umbers, and it was beautiful. Slowly, Marc's mood seemed to lift. Instead of his earlier frown, the hint of a smile now tipped the corners of his mouth. He chewed on his lower lip as he concentrated, and the abstract designs became tiny winter scenes. The last was a laughing snowman with deep-blue skies and swirling snow spinning around the plump little man with a long carrot nose, his hat tipped to the side with a daisy in the band. Marc leaned back and laughed. "There. Kate will be thrilled when I tell her I actually made a snowman."

"Who's Kate?"

"My paralegal," Marc said without looking up, all focus on his art project now. He added, "A friend from work."

"Oh?" he gently prodded for more, but when it seemed he wasn't going to get the story behind the comment, he said, "That's nice."

At that moment it really didn't matter. Marc looked as if he'd found his heaven, his mood now cheerful, which was exactly what Trevor had hoped would happen. Maybe after he was gone, Marc would come down here on his own and put something on that big blank canvas sitting there like an elephant in the middle of the room.

"Let's string the popcorn while all this dries, then we'll fold them into bows for the tree," Trevor suggested. He grabbed the ball of string and unraveled three arm's lengths of it. He snipped it off and handed one end to Marc. They threaded both ends through needles so they could work from the middle out.

"Sure," Marc said, but his gaze was still on the snowman. Trevor couldn't get a read on what Marc might be thinking, but he got the impression Marc wanted to keep painting. If he was right, the door had been cracked, and Marc wanted to open it all the way. *Good.*

"What do you do for fun?" Trevor asked, grabbing a handful of popcorn.

Marc flicked his eyes up, meeting Trevor's with brows raised, and said, "I'm having fun right now."

Trevor smiled and then nudged Marc's knee with his. "I am too, but what else, aside from work?"

Marc's frown returned as he dropped his gaze back to his popcorn-stringing task. "I haven't had time for much of anything beyond work."

"After you make partner, then. What do you *want* to do in your free time?"

Marc shrugged. He looked around the room as if seeing it for the first time. "Maybe I'll paint."

Music to Trevor's ears. "I hope you do," he said. "But I wouldn't wait. Don't let a day go by without doing something that makes you smile or satisfies your soul."

"Spoken like a true artist," Marc said and grinned.

No. Spoken like someone who knows the value of time.

CHAPTER THIRTEEN

"*C*ome enjoy this tree with me," Marc called from the living room, where he was building a roaring fire in the floor-to-ceiling stone fireplace.

Trevor closed the dishwasher door and turned it on before taking one more look around the kitchen. Marc had said to leave the after-dinner cleanup until later, but his mom had raised him better than that. He couldn't leave the kitchen a mess, and he wouldn't let Marc help, either. The man had been gracious enough to offer him his home. Making sure he had a proper Christmas dinner was the least he could do to say thank you.

He made his way toward the couch, but at the last minute decided to sit on one of the large leather chairs that flanked it. Not that he didn't want to share the couch with Marc, but he knew he shouldn't. Already after just one day, the place felt far too much like home for comfort. *Ironic.*

Giving the fire one last stoke, Marc turned, a brief frown marring his handsome face, but he didn't say anything as he sat on the couch—the end closest to the chair where Trevor sat.

"The tree turned out beautifully," Marc said, his gaze fixed on the fire, his voice soft and deep. Trevor felt the rumble of it as if they'd been sitting side by side.

After they'd finished stringing the popcorn, they'd folded their paintings into bows, poked twisted paper clips into them, and hung them on the sparse branches. It was a total do-it-yourself job, but that was what made it the most beautiful Christmas tree he'd ever seen.

"Not bad for a throw-together," he said, suddenly missing his family. The kids would have done something similar, making their own decorations and popcorn strands, and he'd have been right in there with them. He'd called his parents earlier when Marc had been taking a shower before dinner, but it had only increased his homesickness.

"Thank you," Marc said in that faraway dreamy voice of his, the one Trevor was beginning to realize was Marc's wistful if-things-were-different voice.

"For?"

"For wandering into the hotel the other day. For coming home with me yesterday. For everything today. This has been the best Christmas I've ever had." Marc looked over at him, light from the fire flickering like gold in the warm depths of his eyes. "Because of you."

Trevor's heart stuttered and then swelled in his chest as Marc burrowed a little deeper inside, taking up room and claiming a corner without permission. Why did he have to meet Marc now? Why did he have to meet him at all? As if the upcoming months weren't going to be hard enough without meeting someone he could have had a life with.

Marc leaned across the short distance between the chair and couch, bracing his elbows on the arm of the chair, and pressed his mouth to Trevor's. Trevor meant to resist, but there were too many things bouncing around inside him—nostalgia and mourning and longing. Marc's lips felt like fire and home and everything he'd ever dreamed of, and he gave in. Marc raised a hand and cradled the back of Trevor's head, deepening the already-passionate kiss, and for this moment, he could pretend he was healthy, that there could be more, that his mom would get to wear her mother-of-the-groom high heels after all.

They kissed until there was no more air left in his lungs and they had to pull apart, each gasping for breath. Reality rushed back in like a tidal wave, washing away the brief fantasy with it.

"I'm just going to mention this one more time," Marc started, "I promise. But when you get back from visiting your family in Connecticut, I'd like to see you again." His eyes were dreamy and hopeful as he looked up at Trevor. "Say you would too . . . please."

Trevor tore his gaze away and fixed it on the crackling fire. He couldn't bear to shatter that sanguine expression. Or the hope he knew had found a foothold in his own heart, but there was no other choice. "Marc, I . . ."

Marc got up from the couch and kneeled before him, taking one of Trevor's hands in his. "There's something here, between us. I know you have to feel it too. It can't all be in my head. Let's see it through, see where it takes us."

Trevor squeezed his eyes shut, his heart aching for what he wanted but couldn't have. Not for long anyway. He forced himself to meet Marc's eyes. He owed Marc that much while he tried to explain his situation. "Marc, I can't."

Marc opened his mouth, sucking in a breath, but Trevor held his free hand up to stall him. "Please, hear me out."

He nodded and leaned back on his heels, but his grip on Trevor's hand tightened.

"I do feel a connection with you, and I do feel there could be something there . . . if things were different . . . if time was on our side."

Marc cocked his head. "I don't understand."

"I . . ." He took a deep breath. *Best to just rip the Band-Aid off and put it all out there.* "I have end-stage kidney disease. I'm on the waiting list for a transplant, but I've been on dialysis for seven years while waiting."

The color drained from Marc's face and his Adam's apple worked up and down, but he didn't tear his eyes from Trevor's.

"These days people can live longer on dialysis, but less than ten years is still the norm. The day I met you? I saw my doctor that morning, and she told me my kidney function has dropped again. Meaning I'm on seriously borrowed time now." A hollow laugh burst from his chest, and he had to look away. He focused on the fire, the way the flames danced and sang, reaching ever upward. "I've already been living on borrowed time since I started dialysis, but now it looks like my marker is coming due. If a transplant doesn't come through soon, there's a very real chance I won't be alive to see next Christmas. I can't go into a relationship knowing that. It's not fair to anyone. Especially to you."

He risked a glance back at Marc, who hadn't budged. Trevor wasn't sure if he'd even blinked. His stare was so intense and transparent Trevor could practically see every word going into Marc's brain as he processed what he'd just been told. No doubt using that intelligent mind to try to find a way around it, but there was no getting around this.

"No one in your family can donate a kidney?" Marc's voice was hoarse, like it took great effort for him to speak, and a piece of Trevor's heart broke off, scraping painfully against his ribs as it tumbled away.

Trevor shook his head. "Adopted, remember? None of us are a blood match."

"What about your biological parents? Did you try to track them down?"

"Yes, for all the good it did." Trevor had to look away again. The pain and fear and determination in Marc's eyes was too much. "We found my mother, but she was a junkie who'd contracted HIV through sharing dirty needles. Even if we had been a blood match, she wouldn't have been a suitable candidate. And my father was never listed, and she couldn't remember who he was." Once again he whispered a mute thank-you for the family who'd taken him in and called him their own.

Silence fell between them, but Trevor could feel the wheels turning in Marc's mind at hyperspeed.

"I have two perfectly good kidneys," Marc said. He nodded, and determination lit in his eyes. "I want you to have one. We'll go tomorrow and get things started."

Trevor clutched at his chest and fought back tears. He couldn't take this. He turned a watery smile on Marc, whose eyes were shining bright with unshed tears, and caressed his cheek.

"I love that you're willing do that for me, more than I can ever say, but—"

"Please, Trevor. Let me do this. Even if nothing comes of us, I need to know you're out there. Happy and healthy and living a full life." Marc put both hands on Trevor's knees and squeezed tight. "Please, let me save you if I can."

Trevor couldn't hold it back anymore. The tears he'd been fighting broke through and cut a wet path down his cheeks. He shook his head. "It's not that simple."

"Sure it is."

Trevor huffed a moist breath. He could have fallen in love with this man. "An idealistic lawyer. Is that a thing?"

"This isn't funny."

"No. No, it isn't, but tell me, what's your blood type?"

"It's—" Marc frowned. "I don't actually know."

Trevor raised his eyebrows. "How can you not know?"

Marc shrugged. "I guess I never had any reason to find out, but I'll get tested. First thing tomorrow I'll find a lab and get my finger poked."

"Here's the thing, though." Trevor placed his hands over Marc's. "I've been on the transplant wait list for so long because I have a very rare blood type—O negative. Only a little over six percent of the population has it. And the real kicker? Even though my blood type makes me a universal donor, I can only receive blood and, by extension, transplants, from someone who's also O negative. Most people are A or O positive, so chances are incredibly slim that you'll be a match."

"But I *could* be O negative," Marc said, the naked hope in his voice heartbreaking to hear. "Don't discount it until we've made sure."

Trevor shook his head. "The chances that you and I would both have O negative . . . We'd both have a better chance of getting struck by lightning."

"I can't believe that," Marc said with enough conviction to take Trevor aback. "I won't."

"I can't let myself hope," he said quietly, willing Marc to understand. "Even if we're a blood match, that doesn't mean we'll be a tissue match. And say we don't match? Then what? I'll be lucky if I have a year left with where I'm at." He looked down at their joined hands, shaking his head. "No. Hope has been snatched away from me too many times."

"And what if we *do* match?"

"My body could still reject the organ, and I'll be right back where I was. On dialysis but with even less time. Probably with a higher risk of complications, too."

Marc reached up and tucked his fingers under Trevor's chin, gently asking him to meet his eyes. When they did, Trevor's heart broke a little more.

"If we don't match, we don't match," Marc said, his voice low and broken but still commanding. "But that doesn't need to stop us from being together. Wouldn't a year of living to our fullest be worth more than never having had the chance?"

"But that's just it. Don't you see, Marc? We *don't* have the chance," Trevor argued. "It's more than just having to watch my diet every single day, more than having to sit through three hours of being plugged into a machine that cleans my blood every three or four days for the rest of my life. However much is left of it, that is. There's the quality of life, too."

Trevor paused, ran a hand through his hair. He had to make Marc understand. He deserved someone who could give him everything, which started with someone who actually had a life ahead of them. "I'm exhausted more often than not—that's why I needed to nap yesterday. My stomach is almost always unsettled. My sex drive is low—how you've managed to get me so aroused these past couple of days is nothing short of amazing, and has been the most active I've been in years, but it won't last. Eventually you'll end up discouraged and unfulfilled with a partner who can't fully satisfy you in the bedroom or anywhere else, really." Trevor held his hand up, forestalling the argument he saw brewing behind Marc's open-book eyes.

"Bouts of depression bring me so far down sometimes I can't even leave my bed, let alone the house. I can't travel anywhere without first planning ahead to arrange treatments at local dialysis centers. That kind of shoots any spontaneity out the window. Soon I'll probably have to increase dialysis treatments, and then—" His throat snapped closed, and he had to look away before he could continue. "And then I'm just going to die anyway because my blood is too rare to find many transplant donors. The only things on my horizon are the complications that come with this disease, which will end up killing me before my kidney actually does."

But I'll stop dialysis before that happens.

"But every minute of every day would be worth it," Marc said in a broken whisper, and then he rose to his knees and pulled Trevor into his arms.

Trevor's mind resisted, but his heart didn't want to fight the hold. And right then his heart was stronger. He wanted to take this moment for what it was, a beautiful memory he'd been gifted with. He wrapped his arms around Marc, clinging to him for all he was worth, trying to press closer, crawl into the safety of his harbor.

"In another life," he mumbled into Marc's shoulder, the shirt material beneath Trevor's cheek growing damp from his stray tears.

"I can't let you go," Marc said. "Not when I've just found you and there could be so much more for us."

"Please. No more talk." Trevor pulled himself from Marc's embrace and stood up. "This is the way it is—why there can't be more. I have nothing to give you."

CHAPTER FOURTEEN

"That's where you're wrong. You have everything to give me." Marc rose to his feet and took Trevor's hand in his before he could turn away.

How could the man standing before him be dying? Right now? He couldn't accept that. Sure, Trevor had been pretty wiped out yesterday, but Marc, too, was tired after the ordeal of the blizzard and the night of passion. But otherwise Trevor looked healthy as a horse. And to have been told such a bleak diagnosis but still be making sure Marc had a good Christmas, going out of his way . . . No. Marc would do everything and anything in his power to save the man he never knew he needed.

Trevor made to tug his hand back, but Marc held tight. "Come with me. Please."

"Marc—"

He cut him off with a gentle kiss. "Please." He had to know, right now, reassure himself that Trevor was very much alive and healthy and, if he had any say in the matter whatsoever, would stay that way. "You said no more talk, so let me show you."

He led Trevor to the bedroom and stopped at the foot of the bed, turning around to face him. Trevor nodded and let his hands drop to his sides, but his eyes revealed a kaleidoscope of emotion— pain, sadness, longing—his mind a whir behind those blue depths. But lingering beneath it all, there was hunger. That was what Marc wanted right now, to still that mind, draw desire to the surface, and shift Trevor completely into sensation and raw emotion—life in its purest expression.

He placed another sweet kiss on Trevor's silky lips. An air of detachment hovered around Trevor as Marc slowly began unbuttoning his shirt, as though he was just beyond an unseen barrier.

"Let me love you," Marc whispered against Trevor's mouth. "Right here, right now. Let me love you."

Trevor closed his eyes and groaned. "Marc—" His voice was hoarse, ragged.

"Please." Marc kissed him again, soft, reverent, hoping Trevor could understand the words he seemed unable to articulate.

Mere seconds later, Trevor's groan became a moan, and he leaned into the kiss, attempting to deepen it, but Marc pulled back, gentling it until Trevor acquiesced. He had no intention of rushing this. Just like the first night at the hotel with Trevor, that urge to make sure he gave everything he had to this man built like a firestorm in his chest. It mattered more than ever now, as though this was his very last chance at experiencing something great. Something he would never find in his life again. No matter what Trevor said, if they only got a year together, it would be a year to last a lifetime.

With each button Marc freed, Trevor pushed for more, but Marc controlled the pace, their mouths dancing in a sensual give and take. He freed the last button on Trevor's shirt and slowly slid it off his toned shoulders. He ran his hands over the smooth planes of Trevor's chest, his abdomen, up the sides of his torso, and back over his shoulders, cataloguing every inch of the man. All the while, he continued his languid kiss, opening his mouth and teasing out Trevor's tongue, savoring his taste.

His fingers brushed the raised skin of Trevor's biceps. Trevor tensed but didn't break their kiss. Marc did. "This?"

"Direct access to my veins for dialysis." Trevor seemed to hold his breath, his gaze searching Marc's. For what, Marc didn't know, but he wasn't about to stop now. He reclaimed Trevor's mouth, fighting to hold back.

He broke the kiss again and stepped away, shaking his head when Trevor tried to follow. With their gazes locked and the air between them sparking like an electrical storm, he slowly pulled his shirt over his head, letting it fall carelessly to the floor. He moved back to Trevor, wrapping one arm around his back and the other behind his head.

Pressing skin to skin, he claimed Trevor's mouth again, but this time when he deepened the kiss, Trevor answered with a checked fire that Marc fought to keep at bay just a little longer. He wanted this moment, this night, this lovemaking, to last as long as possible. He wanted to draw out every breath and gasp and sensation. Revel in it, roll in it, until it permeated his every pore and became a part of him.

Once again he put the brakes on the kiss, this time having to place a hand on the middle of Trevor's chest to keep him from following. His breath came in short and shallow bursts, keeping time with Marc's. Confident that Trevor would stay put, Marc closed the distance just enough to work Trevor's pants open while holding his gaze, silently telling him that he wasn't going anywhere and that he wasn't letting Trevor go anywhere, either. They would get more than a year because Marc wouldn't have it any other way. He didn't know if he'd be a transplant match, but maybe if he willed it hard enough, begged the universe enough, he would be.

"Stay," Marc said, both meanings intended.

Trevor shook his head. "I can't."

Trevor's pants fell to the floor, and Marc ran a hand down his bare torso and below his navel. He smiled at the harsh intake of breath when he loosely gripped Trevor's filling cock and slid down its growing length. Trevor's eyelashes fluttered, his lips parted, but he held still, letting Marc command him at will.

With his other hand, Marc snapped open the buttons of his own fly and shimmied out of his jeans and underwear. Stepping from the pile of denim and cotton, he pulled Trevor to him, aligning their bodies and marveling at the sweet rush of the contact. This time, when he kissed Trevor, he didn't hold anything back. He couldn't. The restraint he'd been trying to maintain was quickly running out. Trevor answered with fervor, hands cupping Marc's face and angling his head to deepen the kiss even more.

Marc walked backward, keeping Trevor glued to him, until they reached the bed. Only then, Marc ended their kiss once more. "Stay," he rasped again.

"Can't." Trevor crawled onto the bed on his hands and knees. He looked over his shoulder at Marc, who stood at the edge watching him with lust and desire and a deeper emotion he didn't yet know how to name. Instead, he absorbed the sight before him: this gorgeous, generous man who'd come into his life, either by design or coincidence, and tipped it on its side. He never had time for anything but work, but now he begged whoever would listen for all the time in the world to spend with Trevor.

Trevor stretched an arm behind him, hand reaching out, beckoning. Marc climbed onto the bed behind Trevor, and sliding their fingers together, brought Trevor's hand to his mouth. He kissed Trevor's knuckles, turned his hand over and kissed his palm, and then slid Trevor's index finger into his mouth.

Blue fire flared in Trevor's eyes, and he whispered, "Make love to me."

Warmth spread throughout his chest at the words, and he nodded, because words seemed to have left him. Trevor smiled and laid his head to the pillow, one arm—the one with his dialysis access—stretched out in front of him as though he was deliberately keeping it out of the way, and the other tucked under his body. Marc draped his body on top of Trevor, hands gliding over firm shoulders and arms. He pressed a kiss to the back of Trevor's neck, his shoulder blades, then inch by inch down his spine. Lower and lower, tasting, licking, loving . . .

Trevor jumped and moaned when Marc slid his tongue over Trevor's hole, swirled around and in and out, teasing and coaxing him open. Marc's body trembled, his skin flushed with heat, his nerves snapped, and just maybe he and Trevor were creating their own lightning. Trevor moaned again and rocked back against Marc's tongue.

Loving the way this man made his body sing with joy and made him want to scream in ecstasy, he couldn't fathom how anything could be so terminally wrong with him. Marc couldn't wrap his mind around it, make sense of it; therefore, it couldn't be real. In a day or two, Trevor would get his flight home to celebrate the delayed holiday with his family, and then he'd come back, and they would pick up where they left off.

And in reality, you'll probably never see him again.

Marc crushed the voice that spoke what he knew was probably the truth—as much as he refused to believe it—and filled his hands with two well-muscled ass cheeks, kneading, pulling, and pressing, working Trevor's body with his fingers and his tongue, until Trevor's muffled whimpers and gasps told Marc he was on the verge of begging.

"Ready." Trevor grunted. "Marc. Ready."

Spitting on his thumb, Marc used it to caress Trevor's hole, sliding in and out, not wanting to take his hands off Trevor for even the second it took to lean over to the bedside drawer with his other hand. But he did, and one-handed, he ripped open a foil packet from inside, sheathed himself in latex, and then was slicking his aching cock and Trevor's beautiful hole with cool lube. He lined them up and stopped.

"Stay."

"God, Marc," Trevor whined, rocking back. "Please."

"Yes." Marc gripped Trevor's hips, holding him steady while he pushed inside, stretching him wider, slowly filling him, inching deeper and deeper until his whole body shook, inside and out, and Trevor's body clenched and relaxed around his cock.

"Jesus, Trev," Marc growled. "You feel so fucking good."

But if Trevor responded, the words didn't register, all of his focus on the place where their bodies connected, where they had physically become one. Trevor whimpered when Marc pulled back, sliding almost all the way out, and then practically purred when he pushed all the way inside.

"Yes. More. Deeper, harder, faster." Trevor panted, gasped, and chanted it over and over, and Marc would never do anything to disappoint this incredible man writhing and rocking under him.

He gave what Trevor needed—in and out, hard and fast—and the world disappeared as Marc became the eye of the storm. Trevor was the swirling mass of energy and electricity and fire surrounding him, spinning faster and faster, growing too big to be contained in the kinetic clouds. Release came in a booming, blinding burst of lightning. Once, twice, and again. His ears popped, eyes squeezed shut, sweat slicked his skin, and Trevor clamped down on him hard. Together, they collapsed to the mattress, and Marc covered Trevor's body with his own, as though he could be the shield, protecting Trevor from the world, from the reaper who wanted to steal him away too soon.

The storm passed as they floated back down to Earth, and in its wake, it left both of their bodies boneless and quaking in the aftermath. Marc rolled off of Trevor, pulling him into his arms and wrapping his body around him. Trevor burrowed into the embrace, getting even deeper under Marc's skin, and Marc knew this perfect moment of sated bliss was one he'd never have with anyone else.

Marc pressed his lips to Trevor's forehead. "Stay," he said. "Please."

But Trevor had already drifted off and didn't hear him. Or he heard him and chose not to answer. Before Marc could ask again, postorgasmic slumber had its claws in him too, and he followed Trevor into a dream where there was nothing wrong with his kidneys.

Eyes still closed, Marc reached across the bed knowing he'd find an empty space where Trevor's body should have been. That he'd proven himself right didn't do anything to lessen the debilitating disappointment that gripped him in an ice-cold fist. He rolled onto his back and stared up at the vaulted wood ceiling, watching the morning sunrays inch across the room. There was no warmth in the golden light, though, nothing that could fill the heavy emptiness that hung in the air. Had it always been like this? Was he only feeling it now because a brilliant breath of life had blown through the still corners?

He listened for any hint of sound that would tell him Trevor was still there. That right now he was in the kitchen with breakfast prepped, waiting for Marc to wake up. But he knew that was nothing more than wishful thinking. The house was as deserted as his heart felt. He sat up and looked over at a chair by the window, where Trevor's bag had been, but was now only an empty space.

Trevor had left him. Without saying good-bye.

When he could no longer stand lying in bed, he moved through the motions of his morning rituals—bladder relief, shower and shave, dressing. He'd halfway put on his suit before he remembered it was only the day after Christmas—a Saturday—and the office was closed until Monday. Though it wasn't uncommon for him to head to the office on weekends or even holidays, right now he just didn't have it in him.

After swapping his work clothes for casual slacks and a cable-knit sweater—gunmetal gray to match his mood—he made his way into the kitchen. He hadn't realized a small part of him had still been hoping he'd turn the corner and see Trevor there—bright-blue eyes twinkling with delight and a beguiling smile promising everything Marc had ignored on his quest for undeniable success—until the letdown of more empty space weighted his body.

He noticed a plate on the island with strawberries and cubed cheese on it, a glass of orange juice beside it. The gesture brought a touch of smile to his lips, even as it amplified the loss that coursed through his veins. Like a dream he didn't want to wake from. The faster consciousness crept in, the faster the dream slipped through his fingers.

It wasn't until he fully stepped into the kitchen that he noticed a piece of paper beside the plate. With one finger, he dragged the sheet closer to the edge of the counter. Then he carefully picked it up.

Marc,

I'm sorry to leave like this, but it's best this way. You deserve someone whole and healthy who can offer you a full life together. That man isn't me, but I need you to know how much I cherish having met you. I've had one of the best Christmases of my life with you. You've given me a gift to carry me through however many days remain.

I realized there is something you can do for me, though, something that would make me happier than you could possibly imagine. Be true to yourself. Follow your heart and your dreams. Start by going into your art studio and putting something on that blank canvas. Paint something for me. Please.

Always,
Trevor
P.S. Plant our tree.

Marc traced Trevor's name with a shaky fingertip, his vision blurring. *Our tree.* A sob escaped him, and he had to hold on to the counter as he stumbled around the island, trying to sit in a chair before he fell to the floor.

That couldn't be it, could it? No. It couldn't be. He'd told Trevor he wasn't going to let him go, and come hell or high water, he was going to keep his word.

He got up and strode across the room to the hutch where he'd put his laptop when he'd cleared the table for dinner last night. He paused. How could one person have cut through his tunnel-vision-like focus and made such a big impact on his life in so short a time?

Retrieving both his laptop and cell phone, he first searched the internet for local medical labs, only to receive the same message after calling each one: closed for the holidays.

Fuck. His shoulders slumped. *Now what?*

He stared at his phone, as if that would somehow give him the answers he was looking for, and began unconsciously scrolling through his contact list. He paused with his thumb hovering over his mother's name, like he had done countless times before. Only this time was different. She'd given him life, ensured he had a roof over his head, clothes on this back, food in his belly, and an education. She'd fulfilled her parental duty, and the moment he'd reached adulthood she'd washed her hands of him. He'd spent his whole life trying to be someone she could be proud of, but somewhere along the way he'd lost sight of the fact that he never would be.

It took a snowstorm and meeting a random stranger for him to realize he'd been striving for the wrong goal his whole life. And that misguided drive had cost him so much. His mother was gone from his life forever—had been since the day she'd found out he was gay. He just hadn't caught up to the reality. All those years he'd wasted trying to be good enough for her, he'd never been good enough for the one person who mattered all along—himself.

It was high time he did what he should have done two decades ago—wash his hands of her, too. He swiped his thumb over her number, revealing a big red box, and with far more force than was needed, pressed Delete. A surprise wave of triumph washed over him, taking with it all the weight he hadn't realized he'd been shouldering for far too many years.

He tossed the phone on the counter—even that felt good—and his gaze fell on the letter from Trevor again. Relief at finally dropping the albatross around his neck that had been his mother dissipated as a deep sense of loss stole over him. Trevor had just been told he wouldn't survive another year, yet he'd managed to show Marc how much more there was to life in mere days.

Rolling his shoulders back, Marc straightened his spine and walked to the stairs leading to his art studio. He hesitated at the bottom step, taking the room in. It looked different now, *felt* different, and he could only think that was because Trevor Morrison had left a small essence of himself behind. Marc's gaze settled on the corner where they'd sat just the day before, painting and laughing. It had been perfect.

With newfound resolve, he strode across the room and opened a cupboard to pull out a fold-up table. He opened the legs and set it beside the easel, then went back for paints, brushes, and water. He could do this. If anything, maybe it would help bring him closer to Trevor in some odd way.

Brush in hand, fire in mind, and desire in heart, Marc laid down the first brush stroke. And so began his first painting since he was fourteen years old.

CHAPTER FIFTEEN

The day had taken a toll on Trevor. Two days after Christmas, and his morning had started with four hours in airport security lines that led to almost missing his rebooked flight, only to sit on the single open runway for another two hours before they were airborne. Add to that the stress of managing to squeeze in a dialysis session the day before, and then spending another night in a hotel close to the airport, ruminating on his decision to walk away from Marc. It had taken everything in him not to go back yesterday, to hope that maybe this time the odds were better than being struck by lightning and their blood and tissue would match. He couldn't deny how strongly he felt like he'd found a heart match with Marc, but he knew all too well how slim that hope was and how much more it would hurt to lose again this time. No, leaving was the right thing to do.

Was it really?

Yes. Yes it was.

Then why do you keep questioning yourself?

Stop it!

Somebody stick a fork in him. He was done.

A warm hand on his knee drew his attention back to the present—dinner with his family. They'd already celebrated Christmas with the kids but had planned a second celebration for him. His nieces and nephews even rewrapped some of their gifts so they could open them again with Uncle Trevor. God, he loved his family so much.

"Are you okay, *mijo?*"

His throat tightened and his eyes stung at his mom's question and concerned expression. He placed his hand over hers and squeezed.

"I'm good. Just tired. It's been a long few days getting home." He smiled, hoping it reassured her that there was nothing more. She watched him a moment longer, though, her shrewd gaze probably seeing everything he didn't want to say. Not yet. Then she nodded and turned back to her meal. He couldn't broach that subject yet. Not tonight. Not while everyone was in high spirits and enjoying one another's company.

As soon as dinner was over, Trevor excused himself for the night. Though that took nearly another half hour in order to hug all of his siblings, nieces, and nephews. By the time he'd finally made it to his old bedroom, he hardly had the energy to change into his pajamas.

He'd just crawled under the covers when there was a light knock on his door. He knew who owned that quiet request for permission to enter. His mom had never just barged into his bedroom—or any of his brothers' and sisters' rooms—without asking first. It was one of the many small ways she'd taught them respect and manners through example.

"C'mon in, Mom," he said, propping the pillows behind his back and sitting up.

The door opened, and she peeked her head inside the room and smiled. Her dark eyes shimmered with worry as she came in and sat beside him on the bed.

"What is it you're not telling me?" Her voice was soft, but a hint of Hispanic accent remained clear.

Trevor looked into her eyes, which were always so knowing, so empathetic. She was the glue that bound this gloriously mismatched family of his. A family he wouldn't have traded for the world.

Instead of answering her aloud, he pointed to his travel bag on the floor. "There's a zippered pocket on the inside."

She raised an eyebrow but said nothing as she got up, opened the pocket, and pulled out the pamphlet Dr. Wheyvan had given him before Christmas. When she read the title on the front, her shoulders fell and she placed a hand on her chest, as if in an effort to keep herself from tipping over. Or her heart from spilling out. Without looking at him, she sat back down on the bed and a gust of air that might have been a word rushed from her lungs.

When she finally looked at him again, her eyes were swimming with tears. "No, *mi cariño*," she whispered.

"I haven't made any decisions yet. Dr. Wheyvan said I still have time to think about it, to discuss it with you, the family, but I don't really have all that much time. My kidney function is dropping, and before too long even dialysis won't help."

"Oh, Trevor." She sniffed and threw herself into his arms. "*Te quiero, mi cariño.*"

He held her tightly to him, her small body frail but so very strong. "I love you too, Mom."

"I'm so sorry I can't save you from this. Forgive me."

"*Mami*, no . . ." He eased her back enough to look her in her eyes, to make sure she understood. "None of that. You've given me *everything*. The best life a boy could have ever asked for."

She ran her hand over his cheek and gave him a watery smile. "Such a good, strong boy." Then she looked down at the pamphlet now crumpled in her fist. Frowning, she eased her grip and sat up straight.

"Tell me about this?"

For the next half hour he told her everything Dr. Wheyvan had said, that it was his choice and whatever that choice was would be respected. That he'd likely only survive another year without a transplant. That soon the burden of dialysis would become too much to bear, complications would become a factor, and that if he did stop treatment, he'd likely pass within a week, which drew a small sob from his mom.

"She said it's actually a very gentle death," he said, hoping that might give her some reassurance should he decide to stop. "I'll just get really sleepy, and . . . Don't we all want to go peacefully in our sleep, knowing we've lived a good, full life? I don't want to be hooked up to machines trying to squeeze out another day that only hurts to live through."

She nodded. "But you're so young. You can't be done on this earth yet."

"I'm pushing forty," he said softly, attempting a grin that felt lopsided. "You've given me a good life, an amazing family, and I've been loved unconditionally. I've had more accomplishments and successes than I could have imagined, and even inspired a few souls along the way. What more can anyone ask for?"

"Love," she said, and the patched-up pieces of his heart threatened to break apart again.

"I have all the love I need." *Except Marc's.* Trevor managed to keep his voice from cracking, but the words grated over his vocal chords like coarse sandpaper. Even if Marc came to love him, it would be selfish of Trevor to take that love knowing he would only be able to give it back for a short time.

"The love of a man, *mijo*. A man of your heart."

Trevor shook his head, reaching down for a resolve he didn't really want to use. "I can't do that to him."

Her eyebrows rose, and a light sparked in her deep-brown eyes. "Him?"

Trevor sighed and ran a hand through his hair. "I met someone."

She turned, bringing one leg up onto the bed, to sit facing him. "Tell me about him."

He smiled, completely unable to hold it back thinking about the handsome man he'd met by random circumstance but whom he was crazy about. "He's a lawyer, but I think he'd rather be an artist. About my height, dark hair, incredible green eyes, and the most infectious smile you've ever seen. His family was hard on him, I think. He didn't have the love and support I've had. And he's alone, Mom. So alone."

"You must bring him home, then. We'll give him family." She nodded, the matter decided and settled in her mind.

Trevor reached out to hold her hand. "You'd love him."

Marc was just the kind of person she'd take under her wing and make a mission out of making shine, showing him how much he mattered. She was one of those people who made every person she came across feel special, and he so wanted to bring Marc home to meet her.

If you weren't dying.

And once again it came back to that.

A halfhearted laugh surprised him. "Figures, doesn't it? I'd end up meeting someone I could see a future with on the same day I'm told how little of a future I actually have left."

"Maybe you have more time than you think. Maybe the doctor is wrong."

"Mom—"

"It's not right for a parent to bury her child," she said, her voice strained, as if the words she spoke took great effort. "But . . . I can't tell you what to do, *mijo*. The decision must be yours. Whatever it is, we will support you every step of the way. Above all else, I want you to be happy and healthy. If you stayed only to make your mama happy, it would break your mama's heart to see you stay in misery."

She fell silent, letting her words sink in, but they just kept chasing each other in circles. He leaned over to pick up his sketchbook from a cubbyhole in the night table, and flipped through the pages. He stopped at his latest sketch and turned the book toward her.

"This is him?"

He nodded, his throat constricting.

She reached out, letting her fingertip hover just above the surface of the page. "He's a handsome man." She met his gaze, and he smiled, tears of his own threatening to spill over his eyelids. "You're painting him?"

Nodding, he turned the book back around to stare at the sketch. Before he'd left Marc the previous morning, he'd stood watching him sleep, memorizing the swell of every muscle, the angle of every bone, the smooth surface of skin that had felt so good sliding over his. He would take all that, everything Marc had made him feel, everything he felt for Marc, and bring it to life on canvas. Wiping an errant tear from his cheek, he closed the book, hiding the sketch, and returned it to the cubby.

"Mom?" He shored up his courage to ask the one question that had been nagging at him since he first read the pamphlet Dr. Wheyvan gave him. "Do you think stopping dialysis is . . . is suicide?"

"Oh, honey." She pulled him into her arms, her embrace stronger than her stature dictated, and he curled against her. "Not if stopping means allowing a natural passing. Some might think so, but your life isn't theirs."

He nodded, closing his eyes. "I just don't want you to think I'm giving up. I'm not. It's just . . ." He swallowed around the golf ball suddenly lodged in his throat. "In a few months I won't even be eligible for a transplant anymore. I don't want to live whatever days are left doped up to dull the pain, confined to machines. I can't put you and Dad and everyone else through that, either."

"I know, *cariño*. I know." She brushed long bangs out of his eyes and cupped his head to her chest. "We're going to have the best holidays ever. We're going to love and laugh and cherish, and for now, live."

CHAPTER SIXTEEN

"You called in sick. Every day last week." Kate followed him into his office, the accusatory tone in her voice set Marc's teeth on edge.

"Very astute of you," he snapped and immediately regretted it. Just because Trevor had walked away the day after Christmas—ten days ago, not that he was counting—with nothing more than a Dear John letter, leaving Marc suddenly feeling out of control, didn't mean Kate deserved to get the brunt of it. Annoyed with himself, he sat down at his desk and tugged his tie loose.

"Don't be an ass." Kate glared, hands on her hips and fire in her eyes. "Mentally you may as well not even be here today. And now you've lost a case?"

"It's nothing."

"Bullshit."

Did he want to tell her? Yes, he did. Kate was the only person in his life who he *could* tell. The only one he could actually call a friend, even though they'd never taken their friendship beyond the hours of nine to five Monday through Friday. But whose fault was that?

His.

"Enough is enough," Kate said, taking his silence as refusal to fill her in. "What's going on with you? First you take days off, then you come back distracted and distant, and now you're being a cranky bastard. And in the courtroom this afternoon . . . I don't know who was wearing your suit, but that sure as shit wasn't the Marcus Roberts I've known all these years." She tilted her head, a thoughtful expression softening her features. "If I didn't know any better, I'd say you were heartbroken."

Marc opened his mouth, part surprise at her spot-on guess, part wanting to share. Then he quickly closed it. Where did he even start? He leaned back in his chair and stared up at the ceiling, rubbing a hand over the back of his neck. "I couldn't build a snowman."

"What?"

"You were right." He looked at her, attempting to smile, but the effort was too great. "There's more to life than work and climbing the ladder of success, things that matter more than your name on a plaque."

Kate raised her brows. "You *are* heartbroken." She sat in the chair on the other side of his desk and leaned forward. "Tell me what happened."

He hesitated at first but quickly found the words falling from his mouth faster than he could keep up with. He told her about getting stuck on the turnpike, meeting Trevor at the hotel, and sharing the night with him. About spending Christmas together—the tree hunting, the decorating, dinner. He even told her about deleting his mother's phone number once and for all.

The more he talked, the more he wanted to talk, and he went on and on, right up to how he'd found a medical lab open the Monday after Christmas. He remembered how high his hopes had been as he'd driven to the clinic. He'd thought he was going to make a difference, already thinking about what he'd say when he told Trevor the good news. Only, the news wasn't as good as he'd anticipated.

"I was such a fool," he said and looked down at his desk, watching his finger slide a piece of paper back and forth on its surface. The feeling of failure refused to let him make eye contact with Kate. "I was *so* certain I was going to be a match."

A full week had passed since he'd had the blood test, yet even now the weight of that letdown crushed him, as if he were still in the technician's office hearing the results on an endless loop. When the nurse had told him he was type A, as common as they come, she may as well have reached inside his chest and ripped out his heart with her bare hands. He couldn't remember driving home that day or how many hours he'd sat in his living room chair staring out at the Front Range and seeing nothing. He'd failed Trevor, and now the man he never knew he'd needed in his life was gone forever.

"But O negative isn't common at all," Kate reminded him, pulling him from his thoughts with her soft, understanding voice. "The odds were hugely stacked against you."

"I know, but I still thought . . ."

What? That his life would be like some sort of romance novel and he'd magically be "the one"? Of course he did.

Fool.

"You thought you'd be his knight in shining armor and ride in on your big white horse to save him?"

Exactly.

Marc swallowed. "Something like that."

"You don't need to be a knight, Marc."

"That's good, because clearly I'd make a shitty one," he mumbled. He couldn't remember having ever felt so completely helpless. Even when he'd had to leave home and fend for himself, he'd had a driving determination to prove his worth. But now . . . no amount of determination in the world was going to change the fact his blood wasn't a match. All the success, prestige, and wealth in the world didn't mean a thing if he couldn't use it to save Trevor's life.

"There's not a damn thing I can do," he bit out, "and I hate that."

Kate frowned, but he could see the wheels turning behind her eyes. No doubt she was looking at every possible angle for something he had missed, but this was one case for which she'd never find the damning piece of evidence in the thirteenth hour.

Seemingly coming to a decision of some sort, she stood. "Come on." She walked over to the coat rack and gathered his jacket and gloves. "I'm buying you a drink."

"There are no answers in alcohol, either," he said, but he got up from his desk and met her at his office door. He didn't want to go home to an empty house, remembering Trevor's presence in every room, and he sure as hell couldn't concentrate on work.

"No." She handed him his coat. "But that's where we're going to join forces and come up with a plan."

Ten minutes later, Kate led him through the casual surrounds of a neighborhood pub a few blocks from their office. He'd never been inside the building before, having turned down every offer for after-work drinks with his coworkers his entire career. Now he couldn't understand why. How did he think an hour or two sharing a drink and conversation with people would have hindered his chance at partner?

The bar interior was welcoming with its warm lighting, comfortable-looking lounge chairs, and reclaimed-wood walls. The low crooning of Jack Johnson drifted from the speakers as small groups filled the scattered tables and booths—shirtsleeves rolled up, ties loosened, hair let down. The majority of the crowd was comprised of the corporate sect of the area. He recognized a few people from the gym in his office building, but as he followed Kate toward the back of the bar, he noticed one similarity between every person at every table: each was visibly relaxing as he or she talked and laughed and vented. He could see now how an environment like this could help settle the dust of a stressful workday. Maybe he'd say yes when Kate asked from now on. Maybe he'd even make a point of being the one to suggest it first.

She led him to a set of lounge chairs in a semicircle around a country-modern-style table where a few of his fellow coworkers were already sitting, laughing over drinks. All of them had invited him out more than once over the years, and surprise covered their faces when they saw him there. Honestly, if the tables were turned, he'd be pretty shocked to see himself there, too.

"Hold on," Brian, a paralegal, said, reaching into his pocket and pulling out a pair of glasses. He put them on and made a play of jerking back in surprise, his eyes alight with mirth. "Is it really you?"

Gillian, a lawyer, smiled. "Who's got a calendar handy?" she asked. "We need to write this day down."

The other lawyer at the table, Patrick, didn't say anything, just stood up, gave Kate a high five, and made a display of pulling a chair from another table so Marc could join them.

Everyone laughed, and heat spread over Marc's cheeks. But the welcome warmed him in a way he hadn't expected. A part of him wanted to wallow in all things lost, but he wouldn't let it get the better of him. He would never have more of Trevor than the memory of the beautiful Christmas they'd shared by random circumstance, and that would have to be enough. Trevor had told him to live, to *make* the time for what truly mattered. Maybe this, right here, was his new start.

These people he'd spent years working beside were more than just coworkers. They always had been—friends, confidants, people who'd *wanted* his company because they liked *him* just as he was—but he'd had his blinders on too tight to see it. He didn't have to be the most successful; he didn't have to be the youngest partner. He only had to be himself.

So many years he'd wasted.

A wave of sorrow washed over him—cold, oppressive, and threatening to pull him under.

"What are you having, Marc?" Patrick asked, bringing Marc back to the present.

He reached for his wallet as he sat down. "Uh . . . brandy."

"Oh no! I've got this." Patrick held his hands up, his smile reaching blue eyes that reminded Marc of Trevor. Another pang of longing, of mourning struck him hard enough to have knocked him off his feet had he still been standing.

"Thank you," he said.

"I'll have the usual," Kate added, and with a nod, Patrick was off to order their drinks. Marc looked across the table to find two pairs of curious eyes on him, and panic streaked through his chest. This was a mistake.

Kate placed a hand on his forearm as his heart began to race. He met her soft blue eyes, not quite as brilliant a blue as Trevor's. He held back a groan. Why did it suddenly seem like everyone he knew had blue eyes, and how long would they automatically make him think of Trevor?

"Are you okay?" she asked, her voice low enough not to carry across the table.

Not yet. "I'm good." He forced a smile, but from the crease in Kate's brow, he knew she didn't buy it.

"I have to know," Gillian started, and Christ, her eyes were blue, too. "How did Kate manage to get you here when we've tried and failed for years?"

He glanced at Kate and shrugged. "Decided it was time for a drink."

"Oh, come on," Brian, with his beautifully brown eyes, said. "There's gotta be more to it than that."

Fortunately, Patrick returned with their drinks before Marc had to answer. He looked around the table as he placed Marc's brandy in front of him and what looked like a rum and coke in front of Kate. "What'd I miss?"

"We're trying to find out what Kate has over Marc to get him here," Gillian said, anticipation in her voice at the prospect of new office gossip.

Marc glanced at Kate, who looked back at him with a question in her eyes. She raised an eyebrow, and he tipped his head in answer. She graced him with a warm smile before turning to their coworkers.

"Marc met someone the night of the blizzard," she began, and Marc tuned out, taking a sip of his brandy, eyes fixed on the base of an empty glass in the middle of the table. He didn't want to see anyone's expression as Kate revealed his story. He couldn't repeat it again, and it wasn't like any of them could do anything about it. Yet, part of him was oddly relieved by simply knowing they knew what was going on.

"So we need to figure out what we can do to help," Kate said, Marc's ears perking up.

"Unless you can magically change my blood type, there's nothing we *can* do," he said.

The table fell into silent, collective thought, and the chatter of voices hummed steadily just below Ray LaMontagne's raspy, soulful voice as he sang about "the best thing." If anyone could figure out another angle, it would be this team of brilliant minds, but Marc had already been over it. Repeatedly.

Brian snapped his fingers. "I've got it!" He leaned forward, and everyone followed suit. "We'll have a donor registration drive. A lot of events my wife and I do have drives and pledges to raise money for various donations. Why not do something similar?"

"That's a good idea," Gillian said. Patrick and Kate nodded in agreement.

Marc had to admit it was a good idea too, even as a fresh wave of guilt crashed into him. He'd been so fixated on his inability to do anything directly, the thought of actively seeking out someone who could had completely escaped him.

"Those types of things take a lot of time and legwork, though, and from what I gather there isn't a lot of time left," Patrick said, looking to Marc for confirmation.

Marc cleared his throat. "No. Trevor said he'd need a transplant in a matter of months." Could he let himself hope this would work? God, how he wanted to.

"Which means we need something that could reach a lot of people in a short amount of time. A charity event of some sort," Patrick concluded.

"Let's do a free concert!" Kate sat up straight, light dancing her eyes. "Unless I can find a bigger name, my band can headline. I'll see if we can't get a few more groups on board. People can come listen to music, dance, have a good time, get their fingers poked, and sign up to be donors." She turned to Marc, her smile huge and infectious, and Marc felt a shift in his chest, a veil lifting from his mind. "With any luck we'll find a match for your man."

For the first time since Christmas Day, Marc's smile felt genuine. There was a real chance that they could find Trevor a new kidney. They had to.

"Thank you," Marc said through a tight throat, making eye contact with each of his coworkers individually.

Kate put her hand over his and gave it a squeeze. "We'll find a donor," she said, and he found himself believing her wholeheartedly.

But . . .

Marc frowned. "Wait. You're in a band?"

Kate glared at him. "See what I mean, Marc? If you ever left your office, or talked about anything other than work, you'd know this. You'd also know that Patrick got his degree on a baseball scholarship."

Marc looked to Patrick and raised his eyebrows. "You were going to go pro?"

"That's right," Patrick picked up the conversation. "Lawyer was my backup plan for after the big leagues, but I blew out my shoulder before that took off. Now I coach girls' softball."

"And Brian here is a hardcore athlete who competes in Ironman triathlons with his wife," Kate continued. "And they both win! You'd also know that Gillian is a thespian and directs plays at the Denver Arts Club. She's won awards."

"You're missing out, man," Brian said, shaking his head but grinning at the same time. "Kate's a kick-ass singer and her band puts on a killer show. We've all been to see them."

"And you'd know all these things if you weren't so completely driven with work," Kate said, her tone and expression pointed.

Marc worried his lip, heat rising to his cheeks. He'd been suitably chastised and couldn't think of anything to say. What could he say, though? Kate was right. They all were.

"What do you do when you're not in the office?" Brian asked. "On weekends?"

"I, uh . . ." Running the emotional gamut, Marc made a stop at uncomfortable and shifted on his seat. "Go to the gym."

His answer was greeted by four pairs of raised eyebrows.

"And then?" Brian pressed.

Marc cleared his throat. "Work on my cases."

Kate leaned back in her chair, a classic I-rest-my-case pose. "Uh-huh."

"Okay, okay. I get it," Marc said, raising a hand in surrender. "I've been letting life pass me by."

"So what are you going to do about it?" Kate asked.

He glanced around the table at these people, his coworkers, friends he'd been too busy to realize would have been there for him all along, each wearing the same expectant expression. "Organize a concert, I guess," Marc said.

CHAPTER SEVENTEEN

"Can you believe this turnout?" Patrick shouted over the loud music, clapping Marc on the shoulder.

Marc scanned the capacity crowd in Denver's City Park Pavilion, where Kate's band was performing on the small stage. "I had my doubts about actually pulling this off."

The last two weeks had been a whirlwind. The day after the five of them had brainstormed the organ donation drive idea, they had begun putting their plan into motion. Fortunately, with it being the dead of winter and many events being canceled due to the repeated snowstorms, the pavilion wasn't in high demand, and the first available date was much sooner than they'd anticipated. It only took Kate a few days to line up five bands in addition to hers. Getting representatives from a major organ donation center and technicians on site for blood testing had been easy too. They needed all they could get. Marc had sent press releases to the local news and radio stations, and the five of them papered the area with flyers and cold-called every person on their combined contacts list. After that, they could only hope people would show up. And more importantly, that one of them would be the hero who'd save Trevor's life.

"Nah, that's what determination does," Patrick said, grinning.

Marc chuckled. "Would you like a gold star?" he joked, raising his voice to be heard over a driving drumbeat and wailing guitar.

Patrick shook his head, laughing, and he gave Marc a playful elbow in the side. "You can take my offer and join me coaching softball instead."

"I'm still thinking!" Marc couldn't help but smile again, at least a little. Patrick had invited him to assist with coaching his girls' softball team in the spring, even though Marc didn't have a clue how to play the game. Patrick had promised he'd learn in no time. "But I probably will take you up on it."

After the organ drive today, after they hopefully found a match for Trevor.

"Good!" Patrick turned his attention back to the stage.

Marc took a deep, steady breath. Loss and failure hummed steadily through his veins, but a renewed sense of purpose, relief in discovering new friendships, had kept him from slipping into depression. He glanced at Patrick. He really had been missing out on much more than just romantic relationships.

In the past couple of weeks, he'd also become better friends with Gillian and Brian. Both Brian and his wife, Grace, were trying to convince him to give Ironman a go. Marc couldn't wrap his brain around a race that took anywhere from eight to seventeen hours to finish, but maybe he'd try out a short-distance sprint triathlon this summer. Gillian, on the other hand, was subtly trying to get him to audition for an upcoming play, but that was scarier than an Ironman triathlon.

All these people had rallied around him when he needed support most—without question or hesitation, without agenda or condition. They'd invited him into their lives and wanted nothing more in return than his friendship. This was what life was about, and he finally got it. The only thing missing now was Trevor.

Brian materialized out of the crowd, strategically carrying three steaming cups of hot chocolate. He stopped in front of them, holding the cups out. Patrick carefully extracted one, passing it to Marc before retrieving the other for himself.

"Thank you," Marc said, lifting his cup in a short salute and taking a sip.

Brian nodded and then joined Marc and Patrick in watching the show.

"Rocks hard, doesn't she?" Brian said, bopping his head along to the music.

"She does," Marc agreed. He hadn't known what to expect, but Kate and her band had blown him away from the first song in their set. Watching her on stage now, he couldn't believe she was the same person. At work she was a conservative, buttoned-up professional, but there on the stage—clad in a black leather jacket, tank top, short black skirt, and triple-tread biker boots with silver buckles up the side, dark hair loose and wild—she was a flurry of energy commanding the audience with ease. He made a mental note to make sure he never missed a show from this point on. He wondered if Trevor would like her music, too—a thought that led to his internal movie theater playing a preview of the two of them. Trevor standing with his back to Marc's chest, Marc's arms wrapped around Trevor's waist, his chin resting on Trevor's shoulder as the two of them swayed to the beat.

"Marc! Marc!" The sound of his name being shouted drew him from his thoughts, and he turned to see Grace pushing her way through the crowd toward him.

"Come quick!" she said when she reached him, her voice vibrating with excitement. She grabbed his arm and tugged him after her. He shot a confused look at Brian and Patrick, who both shrugged and then followed.

Grace led him outside, across the parking lot, and into one of the two mobile blood labs they'd secured for testing and typing. The four of them piled inside, where a woman sat across from the technician, her back to the door.

"Meet Trevor's blood match!" Grace announced.

Marc's eyes widened. "A m-match?" For a second he couldn't think, the words in his head bouncing around like popcorn in a wind tunnel, his mouth hanging open. The woman turned and looked up at him with warm dark eyes. Familiar eyes.

He remembered Maria Jochens well. He'd represented her in a wrongful dismal case a couple of years back. "Mrs. Jochens?" he said, still in shock.

"Please, you call me Maria," she said and stood to face him.

The wind in his mind downgraded enough for coherency, but speech was still a beat or two behind.

They'd won.

"I— Maria . . ."

She smiled. "When I heard about this drive, saw what it was about and who was running it, I had to come. You helped me get my life back, Mr. Roberts. If it weren't for you, I'd have lost everything. This is my turn to do something for you."

Marc lunged forward and pulled her into a hug. She seemed startled for a second but quickly overcame it and hugged him back just as fiercely.

"Marc," he mumbled into her hair, his throat tight with emotion. "Call me Marc."

She nodded against him.

"Thank you, Maria," he choked out as joy and elation exploded inside. Tears clouded his vision, threatening to spill down his cheeks, but he didn't care. "I will never be able to thank you enough."

"Just knowing I might be able to help your friend live is more than anyone could hope to ask," she said.

They would still need to make sure Maria was also a tissue match, but the first big hurdle had been finding a blood match. And they'd done it.

Marc released her and half fell into a chair near the blood-draw station before his knees gave out and he landed on his ass. He stared up at his friends, all crowded into the mobile lab beside him, and let the tears flow freely. *His* friends. People who didn't judge his worth based on success, position, or status, but who cared because they simply liked *him*.

"I couldn't have done this without you." Marc looked at the people surrounding him—Patrick, Brian, Grace, and Gillian, and Kate, who'd joined them without his notice. And of course, Maria. "Any of you."

"We did it together," Kate said, her voice quiet and smile watery. "That's what friends do."

He nodded, wiping his wet cheeks with the sleeve of his shirt. For the first time in weeks the world around him seemed brighter, as if sunlight blinded him from the inside. They were halfway there.

Now he just needed to find Trevor.

CHAPTER EIGHTEEN

*M*arc sighed, disconnecting the call without leaving a message, and dropped the phone on the cushion beside him. If the first half dozen messages he'd left hadn't been returned, this one wasn't going to be, either. He hadn't been able to find a phone number or direct email address for Trevor, but he had managed to track down Trevor's agent. Not that it had done one bit of good so far, and it'd already been a couple of days.

He leaned back on the couch and stared up at the only wall in the living room that wasn't floor-to-ceiling glass. Hanging there now was a colorful centerpiece—Trevor's original painting of *The Lonely Hour*. On Christmas morning, while Trevor had still been sleeping, Marc had come across the painting at the Boulder Art Gallery during his google-fu quest. He'd told Trevor how much that painting had struck him, but what he hadn't shared was that he'd emailed the gallery directly, expressing his interest in purchasing the painting. Since its arrival, he'd spent countless hours sitting right here on the couch lost in it, imagining the two of them sitting there on that bench, arm in arm, Trevor beaming at him with those captivating blue eyes, smiling . . .

Marc tore his gaze away, grabbed his laptop, and settled it on his knees. He opened a browser and typed *Trevor Morrison, artist* into the search field and hit Enter. He wasn't really sure what he hoped to find this time—he'd already searched what felt like a million different ways—but the sense that time was running out was growing stronger by the minute. He *had* to get ahold of Trevor. Whether or not there could ever be a future for them together, there could still be a future for Trevor.

Scrolling through the list of links to sites he'd visited so often he could recite them from memory, he almost missed a new one. He sat up straight and clicked on it, his pulse pounding like a bass drum in his ears. In the "upcoming events" section at the Flatirons Gallery of Fine Art was an announcement for Trevor's newest and final exhibit, titled The Final Hour.

"Final?" A wave of dread scattered goose bumps over his skin. He skimmed the announcement, too keyed up to take the time to read it through properly. All that mattered was the date of the opening—this coming Friday night—and that Trevor would be in attendance. As would Marc.

The fuck with these nerves! Marc stood in front of the main doors leading into the Flatirons Gallery of Fine Art three days later, fidgeting with his tie, his cuff links, his hair . . . anything to put off actually going inside. Even the chilly night air, alive with dancing snow, couldn't penetrate his nerves or push him through the doors.

Trevor had already rejected him once, but this was different. This wasn't about asking Trevor to give them a chance to be together but about giving Trevor a chance to live, whether they would be together or not.

With a deep breath and long slow exhale, he shook out his arms and pulled the door open. Smooth jazz drifted from the main gallery, along with the low din of hushed voices. He scanned the crowd but didn't see Trevor. Maybe he wasn't there yet. Or maybe he was and had just stepped out for a moment.

God, he better be here.

Walking deeper into the gallery, Marc's gaze caught on a large painting, probably six feet wide, at the far end of the expansive room. The painting had a wall to itself, and it caught his eye for two reasons. One because it wasn't done in Trevor's usual brilliant and bold-colored impressionistic style but channeled realism, and two, he recognized the model. It was *him*.

He found himself standing before the painting without realizing he'd even walked across the room, as though he'd been pulled by some unforeseen force. Right away he recognized the scene as the first night he and Trevor had spent together in the hotel room they'd shared. The first night they'd made love. Marc knew now that's what it had been right from the very beginning. They'd never been just a hookup.

And he couldn't move.

More emotions than he could identify, more than he could contain, flew through him, tugging and pulling at his flesh and bones, heart and mind. Trevor did this. Captured a moment that Marc could not find the right words to articulate. He could only stare in silence.

The painting depicted the darkened room, lit only by snow-enhanced streetlights. A band of glowing light settled over Marc's naked body at rest on the bed. Cream-colored sheets were strategically draped over his waist, and his face was hidden in the shadows. Mostly. Anyone who knew him, who looked closely enough, would know it was him. He'd watched Trevor drawing in the dark that night, before he'd confessed things he hadn't voiced in decades.

"Time," Trevor had said when Marc had asked what he'd been drawing. Marc only now understood what he'd meant.

God, he needed to see Trevor.

Distantly, he registered someone standing beside him. He tried to ignore whoever it was, but the person wasn't moving on, which only increased his awareness and discomfort. He chanced a quick glance and found an older Hispanic woman, a full head shorter than he was, at his side, watching him, studying him. Did she recognize him as the model? She shifted her gaze to the painting for a moment before returning it to him. She smiled, and he couldn't help thinking it was a sad sort of smile, or maybe it was the sadness lurking in the depths of her dark-brown eyes, eyes that he had the strangest feeling usually sparkled.

She turned back to study the painting. "He made me promise this painting won't be sold . . . after."

That's an odd thing to say . . . Then his heart stuttered and a dust storm blasted into his mouth. His throat was so dry he could barely force the words out. "After what?"

This time her smile was definitely sad, and her chin trembled ever so slightly. Even without a proper introduction he had no doubt who

this woman was. He didn't know how, but he couldn't have been more certain of anything in his life. "You're his mother."

She nodded. "He wants you to have this painting." As her eyes began to water, her spine straightened more, and it told him everything he needed to know about this woman. She was strong and would face anything life threw at her head-on and with grace.

"He—" Words tangled up on the back of his tongue, and he had to take a deep, slow breath, shaking his head. It didn't make any sense. "I don't understand."

"This is his last show. These are his final paintings." She glanced around the gallery, but he wasn't sure she was actually seeing the art in front of her. Her gaze was distant, introspective, and then it came to a halt on him.

Trepidation seeped into his chest. "I need to see him," Marc pleaded.

"He stepped out onto the terrace for some fresh air." She reached for him and gently took his elbow. "Come with me."

Trevor pulled the collar of his jacket up higher to fend off the cold. He should have put on a hat too, but he'd needed to get out of the gallery right that minute. He'd been getting an incredible response to the portrait of Marc, which was what he'd wanted, but the memories flooding his mind were becoming too heavy. Regrets of what could have been, if not for time, made it hard to keep his public face on. No one else would follow because it was too cold, and he needed a few minutes alone to recharge.

"Trevor," his mom called quietly from behind him. He closed his eyes and took a breath. He wasn't ready to go back just yet, but it was opening night and he couldn't hide from his patrons for long.

"I'll be there in just another minute," he said, his breath billowing out into the crisp night and twining through the fat snowflakes that fell steadily from the heavens.

"There's someone here to see you."

He sighed. He really didn't feel like talking to anyone right now, which was why he'd come out here in the first place. But not even acknowledging who she'd brought with her would be beyond rude.

Hands shoved into his pockets, he turned and froze midway. Standing beside his mother, looking as heart-stopping and gorgeous as the first time he'd ever laid eyes on him, was the man he hadn't expected to see ever again. His heart swelled in his chest, the night sky grew brighter, and his whole body suddenly felt lighter. In that moment, he fully understood the phrase "the angels sang."

"Marc."

His mom let go of Marc's elbow and walked toward him. She cupped the side of his cheek and placed her other hand on his chest. "He's a handsome man. Let him bring you some joy."

"Mom," he said, warning and pleading infusing his whispered voice. He shot a quick glance at Marc, and when he looked back at his mom, her eyes were shining with banked hope. That Marc was here, that she'd met him, wasn't going to change anything. "You know why I can't."

"I swear, I don't know where you got all this stubbornness from." She huffed and then ran her hands down her blouse, smoothing it. "He seems desperate to speak to you, so listen to him, *mijo*. For me?"

When he nodded his acquiescence, she turned to Marc, placed a hand on his arm, and said something too quiet for Trevor to hear. Marc tipped his head in response, but his gaze never left Trevor. With a quick glance and smile over her shoulder, his mom slipped through the door and left Trevor alone with Marc on the snowy terrace.

Shifting his weight from foot to foot, he ran a hand through his hair, not sure what to say, what he could say. He'd told Marc why he couldn't start anything, and it was true now more than ever. He'd just come off a week in the hospital due to a complication with his condition. It wasn't major, as far as complications went, but it could have been, and before too long there would be more—and *they* would be serious. He'd made his decision.

But looking at Marc now . . . Why did the man have to come here? He was just going to make everything harder. Exactly what Trevor didn't want and had hoped to avoid.

"God, I've missed you," Marc said, his voice low and hoarse, and Trevor's chest tightened.

He closed his eyes. "Don't." He hadn't realized just how much he'd been missing Marc until now. How the hell was he going to go through with his plans now? He *knew* seeing Marc again would kill him in ways his kidneys never could.

"Trevor." Warm breath gusted over his cold cheek, and he snapped his eyes open. Marc stood directly in front of him, and he'd never heard the man move. "Why did you leave me like that?"

Trevor swallowed. "I had to." His gaze locked on to Marc's captivating green stare. So intense, so full of hope and desire and everything he'd ever wanted. "If I didn't, I wouldn't have been strong enough to not be selfish."

"How on earth would staying have been selfish?"

"Because I'm *dying*, Marc." Trevor implored him to understand. Anything between them was doomed. "That's the height of selfishness, and cruel to boot, to start something knowing I'm just going to yank it away. I never want to hurt you."

"But you won't." Marc inched closer, reaching out and running a hand up and down Trevor's arm. His skin tingled in its wake.

"You can't know that."

"Yes, I can." Marc's other hand settled on Trevor's hip, and heat radiated out from the place of contact—downward into his groin, upward into his belly and chest. "I told you I would get tested, and I did."

Trevor's jaw dropped ever so slightly, his eyes wide as saucers. After all these years of praying, after all the disappointments... Could it really be...?

The hand on his arm slid up to rest on the back of his neck, a thumb caressing his jaw, and all the while those green eyes held him captive.

"I'm type A positive," Marc whispered, and Trevor's heart fell.

"Marc—"

"But." Marc stepped closer, pushing the cold from the small space between their bodies. A snowflake landed on Marc's long lashes, clinging for a second before falling and disappearing into a tiny droplet on his winter-reddened cheek. "With the help of some friends, we found your blood match. Not only that but she wants to donate a kidney to you."

"I—" Trevor snapped his mouth shut. What did Marc just say? He heard the words, but processing them felt like trying to push a dull, rusty lawnmower through a hay field. Seven years he'd been waiting to hear those words. Seven years of hope and optimism slowly being chipped away. Seven years, and a man he met only a month ago, by completely random circumstance, found the one thing that could save his life.

"I don't know if there can be an us," Marc continued. "I hope to heaven and back that there will be. I would move mountains for you, Trevor. But whatever may or may not come of us, most of all, I want to know you're out there living and laughing and lo-loving, painting the world in joy. Just so long as you're alive."

Trevor's eyes stung as his chest swelled and his heart pounded a joyful beat. He brought a hand up to cup Marc's cheek, and Marc leaned into his touch, his eyes closing for only a brief second, as if even that was too long to lose sight of Trevor, and then Marc kissed his palm.

Trevor wanted nothing more than to fall into Marc's arms, give in to his selfish desires, but . . . "That doesn't guarantee we'll be a tissue match."

"I know. They have a sample waiting—"

"Even if the donor and I are tissue matches—"

"Maria."

"What?"

"Her name is Maria. I represented her in a case a few years ago."

Trevor shook his head and repeated, "Even if Maria and I are tissue matches, that doesn't mean my body will accept her kidney. Mine could reject it, and then I'll be right back where I was—probably worse—and without another chance."

"Ninety-seven percent of kidney transplants are working in a month."

"So you've done some research," Trevor said, impressed and touched that Marc had taken so much initiative. "What about the seventeen percent that fail by three years? Even if the transplant goes well, I'm still going to be on antirejection drugs for the rest of my life. I'm—"

"Stop," Marc barked, his tone brooking no argument. He held his hand up, opening the space between them, and Trevor shivered from a chill that dove in to fill it. "All I'm hearing is excuses. 'If this goes wrong, if that turns bad.' How about, what if this *works*? How about the man I met in a snowstorm who told me to make time for the important things? Who told me to live and follow my dreams? What is your dream, Trevor? What will make you live?"

He looked away. "I can't hope for my dreams anymore."

"Yes, you can." Marc closed the gap between their bodies again, his warmth like a furnace blast through Trevor's thick jacket.

Trevor met Marc's intense, imploring gaze. Maybe he could.

"Life is uncertain and unfair, but it's also beautiful and meant to be lived as fully as we can," Marc said, his deep voice soft. "If the transplant is successful, you'll have years ahead of you. Isn't that enough?"

Trevor searched those deep-green eyes and realized something his gut already knew: lover or friend, this man would be there for him no matter what. "If."

"If." The smile that lit Marc's face may as well have been the sun itself, the way it blinded Trevor. He pulled Marc tight against his body, so close not even a hair could squeeze between them. Their mouths met in an explosion of heat and passion that felt like pure love and set his every nerve, every sense on fire. Any second now that bolt of lightning would strike them.

Eventually he needed oxygen more than he needed to kiss Marc forever, but he only broke away enough to breathe. Their foreheads rested against each other, noses touching side to side, as they shared the crisp air.

"So let's focus on right now," Marc rasped. "Come home with me?"

Trevor closed his eyes. How many times had he thought about this man since they'd parted? How many times had he wished things could be different? Just maybe . . . his prayers had been answered. But still . . . He leaned back, staring hard into Marc's earnest gaze. "How about we see how the transplant goes first, then maybe we can start with dating?"

"I can live with that," Marc said, peppering him with small kisses. "But say you'll come to my house tonight for a . . . non-date."

"Marc . . ." But Trevor smiled, the first genuine smile since Christmas. And then he couldn't hold it back, and said what he'd wanted to say the second he'd turned to find Marc in the terrace doorway. "Yes."

EPILOGUE

"*W*hy are you so fidgety?" Trevor trapped Marc's hands, stilling them against his chest as they rode in the back of a cab on the way to Trevor's parents' house.

"I have no idea." Marc looked over at Trevor, who smiled at him like he could do no wrong. Marc understood the feeling because he felt the same. That first "non-date" after Trevor's art exhibit had become an extended date, and now, a year later, the wonderment and joy of waking up every day with this beautiful man hadn't lessened. In fact, it had grown.

"You've already met everyone," Trevor said, passing streetlights flickering like blue diamonds in his eyes.

Yes, he had. Trevor's mom and dad had stayed in Boulder during Trevor's and Maria's surgeries and all through their recoveries. All Trevor's brothers and sisters had made the trip out too, and Marc had finally been able to make use of the guest rooms in his too-large-for-a-single-man house. A house the Morrisons had turned into a home, starting with Trevor.

"Maybe because this is the first time I'll be facing the entire family together. Or . . . because I'm entering Morrison home turf."

Trevor laughed and raised their joined hands to kiss Marc's knuckles. "You realize there is nothing more you can do to impress them, right? You saved my life."

"Maria did."

"Because of *you*."

"Because I love you," Marc said softly.

Trevor leaned toward him, a hand sliding dangerously close to his suddenly too aware cock, and whispered, "I love you, too."

Hot breath ghosted over Marc's ear, sending a shiver of arousal racing through his veins.

"You're going to get us in trouble," Marc warned, a smile playing on his lips.

"That's okay. I know a great lawyer."

Marc shook his head and chuckled. "Incorrigible."

"Yep. And you love me just the way I am." Trevor pressed a quick kiss to his lips.

Marc let his head fall back against the headrest and soaked in the man who'd become his everything. "I do. I love you more than I can ever say."

"We're here," Trevor said, tilting his head toward the window beside him.

The cab slowed in front of a large colonial-style home set back on an oversized lot, surrounded by snow-covered trees.

The front door opened and half the Morrison clan, led by Trevor's mom, spilled out onto the large veranda before their taxi had come to a full stop.

Trevor brushed another quick kiss on his mouth. "Ready?"

Marc nodded. "Ready."

Trevor paid the cab driver, and they gathered their things from the trunk as a flurry of voices hurried them along. A good half hour's worth of welcome hugs and cheek kisses later, they put their luggage away in the guest room that had once been Trevor's childhood bedroom. After a quick refresh and change of clothes, they headed back downstairs.

Marc helped set the dinner table, but every time he tried to help in the kitchen, Mrs. Morrison—who insisted he call her Natalia—shooed him out. The dining room was set in an open-concept alcove that was raised up from the living room, and it wasn't until everyone had sat down to the meal that Marc noticed something missing from the large space.

"Where is your tree?" He wasn't asking anyone in particular, but he looked at Mrs. Morri—Natalia.

She smiled and glanced at Trevor, raising an eyebrow.

Marc also turned his attention to Trevor, who sat at his side.

"It was supposed to be a *surprise*," Trevor said, leveling a mock-glare at Natalia before bestowing a smile on Marc that he would never grow tired of seeing. Every smile was a promise, and every promise brightened his life that much more. "I wanted to take you out to a live-tree farm tomorrow. I thought we could pick out a tree and dig it up together. Like last year. A tradition of our own."

A tradition of our own . . .

Marc reached for Trevor's hand and laced their fingers together. His voice was a little shaky when he said, "Every time I think I can't love you more than I already do, you prove me wrong."

Trevor placed a soft kiss on his forehead. "I love you."

"Oh my God," Isaac, Trevor's brother, laughed from across the table. "You're going to make all the women cry."

Everyone joined in on the laughter, but Marc didn't miss Isaac's dark, misty eyes. Knowing he'd been caught, Isaac winked at him.

"You boys just make sure you go early," Natalia said. "The weatherman says a blizzard is on the way tomorrow afternoon. I don't want you two getting caught up in it and getting stranded out there."

Marc met Trevor's gaze, and they both smiled. Worse things could happen.

Dear Reader,

Thank you for reading L.C. Chase's *A Fortunate Blizzard*!

We know your time is precious and you have many, many entertainment options, so it means a lot that you've chosen to spend your time reading. We really hope you enjoyed it.

We'd be honored if you'd consider posting a review—good or bad—on sites like **Amazon, Barnes & Noble, Kobo, Goodreads, Twitter, Facebook, Tumblr,** and your blog or website. We'd also be honored if you told your friends and family about this book. Word of mouth is a book's lifeblood!

For more information on upcoming releases, author interviews, blog tours, contests, giveaways, and more, please sign up for our weekly, spam-free newsletter and visit us around the web:

Newsletter: tinyurl.com/RiptideSignup
Twitter: twitter.com/RiptideBooks
Facebook: facebook.com/RiptidePublishing
Goodreads: tinyurl.com/RiptideOnGoodreads
Tumblr: riptidepublishing.tumblr.com

Thank you so much for Reading the Rainbow!

RiptidePublishing.com

 RIPTIDE PUBLISHING

ACKNOWLEDGMENTS

Huge thank-yous are in order for some dear people who've helped me through the writing of this book, but most of all for their friendship and constant support: MC, Alec, Thorny, Anne, and Taylor. I love you guys!

A big toast to my editor, Danielle. You rock, lady!

To my readers, as always, thank you for taking this journey.

Consider becoming someone's hero, and register as an organ donor. You could save a life. Please visit one of the organizations below for more information, or look for a center near you:

Canadian Transplant Association
www.organ-donation-works.org/english/about-us

The Kidney Foundation of Canada
www.kidney.ca/organ-donation

American Transplant Foundation
www.americantransplantfoundation.org/about-transplant

National Kidney Foundation
www.kidney.org

Mayo Clinic Transplant Center
www.mayoclinic.org/departments-centers/transplant-center

also by
L.C. CHASE

about the
AUTHOR

Cover artist by day, author by night, L.C. Chase is a hopeless romantic, free spirit, and adventure seeker who loves hitting the open road just to see where it takes her. After a decade of traveling three continents, she now calls the Canadian west coast home. When not writing sensual tales of beautiful men falling in love, she can be found designing book covers with said beautiful men, drawing, horseback riding, or hiking the trails with her goofy four-legged roommate.

L.C. is a two-time Lambda Literary Award finalist for *Pickup Men* and *Pulling Leather*; an EPIC eBook Awards winner for *Pickup Men*; an EPIC eBook Awards finalist for *Let It Ride* and *Long Tall Drink*; Bisexual Book Awards finalist for *Let It Ride*; and an Ariana eBook Cover Art Awards winner. She also received an honorable mention in the 2012 Rainbow Awards for *Riding with Heaven*.

You can visit L.C. at www.lcchase.com.

Enjoy more stories like *A Fortunate Blizzard* at RiptidePublishing.com!

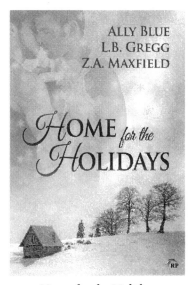